THE ORDER OF THINGS

THE ORDER OF THINGS

KAIJA LANGLEY

Nancy Paulsen Books

Nancy Paulsen Books

An imprint of Penguin Random House LLC, New York

First published in the United States of America by Nancy Paulsen Books,
an imprint of Penguin Random House LLC, 2023

Copyright © 2023 by Kaija Langley

Nancy Paulsen Books & colophon are trademarks of Penguin Random House LLC.
The Penguin colophon is a registered trademark of Penguin Books Limited.
Visit us online at PenguinRandomHouse.com.

Library of Congress Cataloging-in-Publication Data
Names: Langley, Kaija, author.
Title: The order of things / Kaija Langley.
Description: New York: Nancy Paulsen Books, 2023. | Summary: Eleven-year-old April must come to terms with the sudden death of her best friend, Zee.
Identifiers: LCCN 2022053852 (print) | LCCN 2022053853 (ebook) |
ISBN 9780593530900 (hardcover) | ISBN 9780593530917 (ebook)
Subjects: CYAC: Novels in verse. | Best friends—Fiction. | Friendship—Fiction. | Grief—Fiction. | Music—Fiction. | Single-parent families—Fiction. | Lesbian mothers—Fiction. | City and town life—Fiction. | African Americans—Fiction. | LCGFT: Novels in verse.
Classification: LCC PZ7.5.L355 Or 2023 (print) | LCC PZ7.5.L355 (ebook) | DDC [Fic]—dc23
LC record available at https://lccn.loc.gov/2022053852
LC ebook record available at https://lccn.loc.gov/2022053853
Printed in the United States of America

ISBN 9780593530900

1st Printing
LSCH

Edited by Stacey Barney
Design by Eileen Savage | Text set in Celestia Antiqua

For Lanita, whose love and light is
the greatest I've ever known.

THE ORDER OF THINGS

PART I

A Band of Two
September 6

Four Pounds, Seven Ounces

is how I came into the world,
April Janelle Jackson, three
weeks early, not a Mother's
Day baby as expected, but a
preemie.

No longer than Mama's
open hand, no heavier
than a glass paperweight,
fists flailing, lungs screeching
because I'm a fighter.

The NICU nurses said
I was the noisiest baby
in the unit, screamed
every time they changed
a diaper, removed a tube,
placed me in another incubator.

I came into the world a
loud child demanding to
be heard, but you'd never
know that now.

The Sound of Music

makes everything better,
even the first day of school.

In the quiet of morning, there's
no mistaking the faint sound of
a violin, my best friend, Zee,
playing at this early hour.

We're both going to school
today, but not the same one,
not anymore.

Last night I dreamed I was
playing drums on a stage
with a band before dozens
of fans with fingers snapping,
heads nodding along with my beats,
the dream so real I woke up with a jolt.

The only thing better than
listening to music is playing it.

Wash, Brush, Dress

in my school uniform
with the crisp collar,
skirt pleats poppin',
creased shirtsleeves
sharp enough to cut you,
like Mama taught me.

I double-check my ponytail,
every strand in place, grab
my bookbag, my drumsticks,
and ease into the kitchen.

Devour the orange-cranberry scone
Mama baked special for today.

I slip into her
room for a kiss,
but don't wake her.

Her UPS badge on
the dresser, her head
half beneath the pillow.

Working night shift
loading trucks means
Mama sleeps most of

the day, works most of
the night, and we live
in the quiet moments
in between.

Like Clockwork

Zee waits for me in the hallway
outside his apartment, across
from my own.

He's dressed in a burgundy polo,
a gold-and-blue crest on his chest,
khaki pants, new black loafers.

The hallway reeks of fried eggs
and onions, strong coffee and
cologne. Zee has one leg
kicked behind him on the wall,
his violin case in his hand, his
face as hard as stone.

Zee closes his eyes,
takes three long, deep
breaths but still no words.

He's usually not this quiet.

You okay, Zee?

We gabbed all summer about
today, so I know he's as excited,
and as nervous too, as I am.

His eyes open when Papa Zee
exits their apartment,
door slamming behind him,
shirt untucked, hat on backward.

He's late to work today but still
plants a kiss on our foreheads
before ushering us to the elevator.

He jabs the button so many times I'm
afraid it might break. We're only
on the twelfth floor, but the elevator
always seems slowest when we're
in a rush.

One for the road? Papa Zee asks, winking.
How do you make a bandstand?

How? I ask.

Zee leans forward,
fully alert.

You take away their chairs!

Zee laughs out loud.
A real laugh, a belly laugh.

The mood lighter now, the
elevator arrives.

Let's get a move on, Papa Zee says,
letting us enter first.

It's Been

Zee and me forever,
same walk to the same school,
same classes, same teachers,
until Papa Zee promised when
the new Boston STEAM charter
school with a focus on the arts
opened in the neighborhood,
Zee could audition.

It's been six months since and
I still don't feel prepared.

You scared? I ask, falling in step with Zee.

At least we still get to walk together
most of the way, our schools only
five blocks apart.

Not scared. Can't believe it's literally happening.
I'm already good, you know?

Good is an understatement.
Zee is a violin prodigy.

I'm nowhere close,
but I want to be better.

Me too, Zee. Me too.

Zee doesn't miss a beat,
stopping short to face me,
giving me his full attention.

He smiles so big,
both dimples show.

I knew you wouldn't give up!

I feel my face burn, a reminder of
three failed lessons with teachers
I never have to see again.

You still think tonight is a good idea, right?

The best, he says.

We start walking again.

*You're going to this fancy new school.
I can't have you leaving me in the dust!*

Me? Never. You and me, always.

He offers me a fist bump.

We're the only kids on the block
now, which can only mean we're
late or about to be. It's like we
read each other's minds.

We take off running, his longer legs
pumping harder, pounding down the
sidewalk, violin case flapping at his
side. I'm on his heels the entire way.

When we reach the intersection
where we've never parted ways
before, we're both out of breath.

You going to be okay without me? he asks, gasping.

Do I *have a choice?* I pant back.

When the light turns green,
he goes left, I start right and
do my best not to peek back at him.

Zander Elliot Ellis Jr.

is Zee for short—never loud, or
rough and tumble, hard or fast, or
the clown of the class—just Zee.

Because he's a junior,
saying *Zander* means
Daddy and son both
turn with those same
big eyes, broad nose,
velvet-brown skin,
with a smirk on
their lips, a question
in their eyes.

We were born a month apart,
but Zee was twice my size
even as babies, but no match
for my energy in the
playpen where we
cried . . .
wrestled . . .
cuddled . . .
each other before we
crawled . . .
walked . . .
talked.

Zee is more than
my best friend, he's
like a brother. He's
family.

We're bookends.
We are.
I'm the A to his Z.

Fast-Walking
to school, feeling alone
and unprepared for a year
without Zee and me passing
notes in class, sharing lunch,
ignoring games on the playground.

It's a small comfort to hear music
all around me as I near school.

A woodpecker in a tree, the construction
worker across the street, beats everywhere.

I'll at least be thankful for that.

Sixth Grade Is Off

to a rocky start when I walk into
homeroom and everyone huddles
near the doorway, shocked to find
the desks have already been assigned.

So much for hiding in the back of
the classroom like I did with Zee.

This year seating will be organized by first names,
says Ms. Chisholm.

The twins, Theo and Thea, fist-
bump and find their seats near
the back of the room.

Mercy, Mimosa, and Merilee run to
their new desks nearest the bulletin
board, giggling all the way because
they've been inseparable since
second grade.

The rest of us grumble as we look
for our desks, still shaking off the
last bits of summer.

Settle down now. I promise it won't be that bad.

I bounce in time to the rhythm
in my head as I find my name
on a desk nearest the window.

The one next to mine has the name
ASTREA "ASA" CURTIS.

On cue, Asa arrives after the second
bell, her white shirt wrinkled, collar
mustard-stained, socks two different
blues.

The room fills with the scent
of campfire smoke and pine,
like she walked to school
through a forest, her gaze landing on
the empty desk beside me.

She says in her outside voice,

*Sorry I'm late. Missed the bus.
Had to walk. What did I miss?*

No one replies as she stomps
across the front of the room and
falls into her chair with a thump.

There are only three white girls
in class and the other two give
each other looks, shake their heads,
turn their attention toward the teacher.

There's No Mistaking

of all my classmates, Asa
is the most like an open
book you didn't ask to read.

You never have to guess
what she's thinking because
she's going to tell you, then share
all your business, and she's been
that way since the first grade.

All morning, Asa keeps leaning
in my direction, keeps asking a
dozen different ways what I did
over the summer.

I know she's only asking because
she wants me to ask her about her
summer, and I honestly don't want to
know.

I tap out a new beat on my desk—
tap, tap, pause, three fast taps—
to drown out her words, to distract
her. I quit when I get a look from
Ms. Chisholm telling me without
words to stop.

The class is restless long before the
lunch bell, whispers and note passing
around the room are anything but quiet.

Ms. Chisholm clears her throat to make
an announcement, and I'm hoping it's
not any worse than her getting creative
with the seating chart.

This year we'll have multiple class projects
that will require students to work in pairs.

Hands down I would choose Zee, but I
scan the room for other classmates who
might not be too bad.

Starting with the students nearest the windows,
today you will work with the classmate to your right.

That means Asa. I tap out a beat
on my desk to calm my nerves.

After lunch, you'll each share the answers to three questions:

What do you like about your name?
What's your favorite food?
What is one goal you want to accomplish this year?

When the bell rings, I make a dash
for the door, but not fast enough to
escape hearing Asa's voice over the
noise of two dozen sixth graders clamoring
for food.

See you later, partner!

When the Clock Strikes

noon, I scramble to find
a corner of the playground
all to myself, away from the
shrieking voices, kids' legs
and lungs stretching.

I use my free time to tap out a
combination on the cement with
the sticks Papa Zee gave me.
It took me two years to admit
I wanted to play, and another four
to get up the courage to ask Mama
for lessons.

Papa Zee offered me lessons once,
but I didn't want the pressure of needing
to be as good as Zee.

Asa wants to know what I did
this summer? I took drum lessons.

The first teacher wasn't patient,
the second wasn't kind, the third
said I had no talent, which almost
made me change my mind.

Almost.

Each time I told Mama
I didn't like the teacher,
and to be honest, I think
she was relieved.

Mama's not so keen on all that
clickety-click-boom-bang
of drums under her roof.

Still, I've never stopped wanting
to play or have a drum set of my own
or be in a band one day.

Class Project #1:

everyone pairs off, desks facing
each other to share the answers
to the three questions.

Asa can't wait to start.

*My daddy named me Astrea. He said it means star. My favorite place
in the world is to be under a night sky watching the stars, but you
can't see them so much in the city. Which is why we go camping.
A lot. I love s'mores because there's nothing better around a campfire,
even if it's only in our backyard. Oh! And I want to get my last badge
before Girl Scouts next summer. I think that's it. Your turn.*

Ms. Chisholm weaves between
the desks, nods at me to talk
with Asa.

*It's cool to be named April because that's when I was born.
I love all fruit, but never in dessert.
I'm still figuring out what I want.*

A whole year ahead with Asa,
who shares everything,
means the less she knows,
the better.

This is the first time I've really
looked at Asa. She's taller and lankier
than me, with long brown hair and hazel
eyes, while I'm short, thick, and the color of
red clay.

That's not where the differences end.

I know she also has two parents
at home, lives in a single-family house,
has two younger siblings.

It's just Mama and me,
Zee and Papa Zee, in an
apartment tower on steroids.

Maybe this year won't be so
bad without Zee, but I'm not
counting on it.

The Last Bell

can't come fast enough,
and I rush out the room,
bumping into Mrs. Dial,
my fifth-grade teacher,
in the hallway.

Sorry! Going to meet Zee.

In no time I'm back at the
intersection, and instead of
Zee solo, there's a pack of
students walking with him,
laughing, talking, joking
about their day.

Zee waves me over.

Come meet Josh, Randy, and Lamar.
This is my best friend, April.

Two carry violin cases, one has a large
hard case that might be a saxophone,
or a trombone. The shortest boy
with the bowlegs pipes up.

You play too?

April plays the drums, Zee says proudly.

The three boys give me a look
like that can't be true, but I don't care.

Ready to go, Zee?

Zee waves goodbye.

My best friend just told a bunch
of strangers something I haven't
yet had the courage to say myself.

This All Started

six Christmases ago
under a real tree that
Papa Zee wrestled up
twelve flights of stairs
because it wouldn't fit
in the elevator, him still
in his postal service uniform,
trailing needles everywhere.

A violin for Zee and a drum set
for me. It took no time at all for Zee
to start plucking at the strings with his plump
fingers, no bow in sight, single notes
that didn't sound like much at
first until the melody for a song
we all knew—"Twinkle, Twinkle,
Little Star"—floated through the air.

Zee may be a prodigy, but his
musical roots run deep with
Papa Zee a drummer, his mom
a blues fiddler.

Though neither one of us has met her.

I jumped on the drums, making so
much noise in the shelter of Zee's

apartment that Mama covered her
ears and shook her head.

I was always tapping, making
beats with my fingers and hands
on tables, desks, and walls, but real
drums was next level for us both.

So, that's where the drums still live.

Until now, Zee has been the star musician
in our family, but that's about to change.
I've waited this long for my turn, and that's
plenty long enough.

Dreaming Aloud

is what we do to hype
each other up, ever since
my first lesson this summer.

I can tell Zee feels good because
when he's happy, there's a bounce
in his step, like he's floating on clouds
down the street.

We pass an ice cream truck,
jingle blaring, kids yelling orders
and dropping change on the ground.

We should celebrate our first days, right?

Zee pulls a few crumpled bills from
his backpack, buys an ice cream
sandwich and a firecracker pop.

I savor my sandwich while Zee
gobbles his pop in three quick bites.
The sugar rush hits us at the same time
and he starts . . .

I'm going to be first chair for the Boston Symphony Orchestra.
The first Black violinist to lead the BSO
in its 141-year history. I'll get you tickets.
Put you on my special guest list too.

He nods at me, telling me it's my turn,
and I go for broke not holding
anything back.

Ha! That's if I'm in town! I'll probably be on tour,
on a stage, thirty thousand people stomping their feet
to my backbeat, my sticks moving so fast you
can hardly see them in the nosebleed seats.

Zee claps his hands, egging me on like
I'm already onstage, my loyal cheerleader,
my best and only true friend.

When we reach our building,
we slap hands, Zee winks,
clinching the deal, setting
our dreams afloat.

Word.

The Moment

the elevator doors open on our floor,
the blissful scent of baked
bread and cloves fills the hallway.

Mama bakes all kinds of things,
rolls and loaves, cookies and
croissants, muffins and buns,
making my mouth water each time.

I high-five Zee goodbye for now, slip
into my apartment like a whisper.

I kiss Mama hello in the kitchen,
where one loaf is cooling, a second
prepared for the oven after the ham
is done.

Good first day? Mama asks, giving
me a once-over, making
sure I was presentable in the world.

Good enough, I guess.
Super weird without Zee.

I settle at the table to watch her work,
her copper skin damp with sweat,
her baby locs covered
in a silk rainbow scarf.

We have the same high
cheekbones, jet-black eyes.

The pages of the cookbook she's
using are worn at the edges, held
open with a ruler.

I can imagine. Change can be hard.
You like your teacher?

I guess so. Too early to tell.

Our brick building is hot all year long,
nice in the winter, but right now the
entire apartment feels like an oven
only six days into September.

Thanks for the scone this morning.
So yum! Anything I can do?

Mama pinches my cheek
before digging her hands
into polka-dot oven mitts.

Get ready for family dinner.

She removes the ham, inserts
the second loaf. One we'll keep,

the other we'll take for dinner tonight
with Papa Zee and Zee.

Mama bakes so many things,
shares them with neighbors,
friends at work, but mostly she
bakes for us.

I'm always grateful because
Mama bakes love.

The Order of Things
in my life is simple:

quiet and efficient,
calm never commotion,
just as Mama likes it.

Like putting on socks before
shoes, letting dough rise before
baking, kissing Mama good night
first thing in the morning.

It's important.

We keep our voices low, the
television off, even our alarm
clocks don't beep because we
never set them.

There's nothing except books
and magazines to distract us
when most people have a
television going 24/7,
reality shows or news,
but Mama has no patience
for either.

I asked Mama once why
we live the way we do.

Warehouse work is noisier than you can imagine.
And don't get me started about what it was like in the army.
Silence is golden. It is music to my ears.

A quiet home is a small sacrifice
to keep Mama happy, but wanting
to play the drums makes me
a round peg in a square hole,
always out of place.

My Room

is my safe space, which Mama
only enters twice a week when she
empties my trash, gathers my
laundry, and returns it smelling
like a spring breeze for me to
iron, fold, and put away.

Clothes in the closet,
shoes beneath the bed,
textbooks in a stack on
my desk, my drumsticks
in the windowsill.

I change out of my school
clothes and fidget with my
drumsticks, the weight of them
in my hands making me more
excited as I tap out silent
beats on my bed.

Tonight couldn't come fast
enough, and I'm prepared
with an airtight case.

The creak of the oven door
tells me the second loaf is
done, and I'm ready as ever
for family night.

Every Tuesday

Mama and me cross
the hallway to join
Papa Zee and Zee
for dinner and dessert.

We arrive to sounds of
pots clanging, a jazz band
streaming from Papa Zee's phone.

There's always music in the
Ellis household. Jazz and blues,
hip hop and soul, sometimes reggae,
sometimes classical. And nothing is orderly.

Not the old newspapers, sheet music
everywhere, or clean clothes
dumped on the sofa where I sleep when
Mama goes to work.

Beige egg-crate foam pads the walls to
dampen the sound in an apartment
that looks lived in, feels wallowed in
whatever's going on that week.

I glance at the drum kit in the corner.
Zee follows my gaze, gives me a nod.

I've been waiting on you two to share my latest.
Ready? Papa Zee asks.

Papa Zee's bad jokes are bad, but secretly
I like them. More than his jokes, it's hard not
to be in a good mood around a man who
looks like Black Santa and plays one
at the local mall every Christmas.

Are we ever ready, Zander? Mama chuckles.

She places our dishes on the cluttered
dining table, hugs them hello.

Why did the pianist keep banging his head against the keys?
Anyone?

Crickets.

He was playing by ear.

Dad, Zee teases, *don't quit your day job.*

And we laugh, the mood happy and light.

Papa Zee dances as he cooks, his
apron strings flapping behind him,
hands wet from washing and chopping
the lettuce and veggies for the salad.

Zee grabs the plates from the cabinet,
I get the glasses. We take turns racing
to clear the table, get the places set for dinner.
I act like I'm not listening to Papa Zee and Mama
each time I go back to the kitchen, but I am.

Chantelle, we aren't getting any younger.

What about you? Mama's brow pinches together.
Might do you some good.

*You kidding me? All my money and time go to him.
Plus, he's eleven going on grown. Seriously, invite her.*

Invite who? I ask, stepping into the kitchen.

*Never you mind. Take this bowl over to the table,
please.*

I pause, waiting for either of them to say more.
Both stare at me with blank expressions before
I join Zee at the table to fuss over the napkins.

Mama and Zee settle into one side
of the table, Papa Zee and me on the other.

I keep waiting for the right moment to
speak up about my idea, but the
time never seems right.

Papa Zee and Mama ask Zee lots
of questions about his new school.

Are the teachers nice? Mama asks.

So far everyone is nice, Zee responds.
Make any new friends? Papa Zee wants to know.

I *met some cool classmates, but I already have a best friend.*
Zee nudges me with his foot.

I don't mind all the attention
on Zee because I'm suddenly
nervous about my plan.

After dinner, I steady my voice to speak.

I *have something to share too.*

Zee shifts to the edge of his seat, ready.
He's already nodding his head in support,
and I'm still mustering the courage to speak.

I know the drum lessons didn't go so great this summer.
But I have a better idea, I think.
Papa Zee, you still available to teach me?

Papa Zee's face lights up in surprise,
then excitement. He pulls me in for a side
hug. Zee reaches across the table to shake
my hand, like something formal just happened.

I wasn't so worried about
Papa Zee, to be honest.
After all, he gave me his
old drumsticks.

After We Cross

the hall, standing face-to-face
in our kitchen, I promise Mama
I'll really try this time. I will.

I'm there most nights anyway
when Mama goes to work.

I'll *keep my room clean* (already do),
fold my clothes (what else is new),
I'll *even wash my own clothes once a week!*

Across the hall I can hear Zee
warming up his violin while Mama
taps her foot, but stops me before
I dig myself in too deep.

Okay, April. If you're going to do this, don't waste Zander's time.
Don't take advantage. Please show up and make it count.

I hop from foot to foot, excited.
The corners of Mama's lips turn
up, despite herself.

And before you get any ideas, the drums stay with Zander.

I give her the biggest hug.

I've Got a Feeling

when I wake up that there's
nothing to hold me back now,
it's smooth sailing from here.

At least I hope so.

I join Zee in the hallway and he
nearly tackles me hello he's so
excited.

You did it! That was perfect!

I wait for the door to open, the blur of a
blue postal uniform to appear, but no Papa Zee.
Then I remember he was late yesterday.

Guess there's no turning back now.
Maybe I should have asked him earlier?

Zee straightens his tie,
adjusts his blazer, his face
a mop of wetness.

All that matters is you asked him.
It's going to be great, wait and see.
Know what else?
I hate this uniform.

I offer to carry his backpack.
He looks so miserable in the
stuffy elevator and not much
better when we reach the street.
It's eighty degrees outside and
a blanket of humidity.

As we start our walk to the intersection,
he has less bounce in his step than yesterday.

For real, is the new school okay?

Now he's walking even slower,
dragging his feet like he doesn't
want to go to school.

It's going to be harder than I thought, he says.
Classes and music in the same place.
The other kids are good too.
I feel like I've got to prove myself.

Zee, who can play the hardest songs, who
has never doubted himself and has always
been my musical hero, has to prove himself?

It's only the second day of school.
You'll have them cheering in no time.

Nobody plays, or practices, like you.
Nobody. You're one of a kind, Zee.

Okay, okay. Do you really think so? he asks, eyebrows raised.

I *know so.*

Zee wipes his face on his blazer sleeve,
gives his whole body a shake, and his mood
shifts. I hand him his backpack with
only five blocks to go.

You're right, I can do this. They'll see.

And if they don't? I ask to make sure he's okay.

I'll just work harder than everyone else.

Zee gives me a side hug before
breaking into a sprint across the
intersection. Today, I wait until
he's out of sight before I leave.

How Could I Forget

yesterday I was matched
with Asa as a project partner
and now there's no escaping her.

I haven't been in my seat
five minutes yet when Asa
arrives and starts talking
like we were already
having a conversation.

I miss summer already. Don't you?
It's too hot to be sitting in a classroom.
You figure out what you want yet?
You didn't know yesterday.

Ms. Chisholm writes the announcements
on the board because the intercom is broken.
Even though the window is open, there's no breeze.

If I tell you, will you keep it to yourself?

Ms. Chisholm turns to see who's talking.
We both sit up straight in our seats.

Ooh, tell me please, Asa says, lowering her voice.

If I don't tell her, I know she'll keep asking.
I won't last the week, much less the year

without begging Ms. Chisholm to rethink
the seating assignment.

I want to play the drums, be in a band.
Might even go on a world tour one day.

Asa's face lights up.

That's amazing! How cool would that be?
I've been to twelve national parks, but we've
never left the US. Aren't you scared?

I'm terrified.

What if I'm no good, like that teacher said?

I've never left Massachusetts, but my mom did
a tour in Germany, South Korea, and served in
Afghanistan. If she can travel the world, so can I.

Mama's army uniform looks as good as it
did the last day she wore it, before the calling,
the urging, the gnawing she could no longer
ignore told her it was time to be a mother.

A different kind of duty, she'd said,
and we started our journey to each other.

What does your dad do?

This is why I keep to myself at
school, why I miss Zee so much.

I tell her Mama is single by choice.

She doesn't date men.

April turns crimson, starting at the tip
of her ears, spreading across her face.

She doesn't say anything else
for the rest of the day, and that's
fine by me.

Take Two
with Zee after school,
today he's by himself.

We survived another day! Zee says.

He strips away his tie, shoves
his blazer into his backpack. He can be
so dramatic sometimes, making it seem
like school is hard, but Zee excels in school
the same way he does with the violin.

How's it going for you? he asks.

I tell him about Asa, about her not
knowing or remembering about Mama.

Seriously, though, she's not so bad.
Didn't flip out when I told her about the drums.
Or go telling everybody who would listen.

That's a win. I met my music teacher today.
Mr. Sanderson went to Juilliard for violin.
He plays multiple instruments too and
was in a high school band that traveled
as far as Florida during summer tours.
That was all a long time ago.

I've never been envious of Zee or his talent,
but I feel a moment of regret that I didn't try
harder with the drums sooner.

He sounds cool. You'll probably learn a lot from him.
Does he offer drum lessons?

Zee cocks his head to the side,
a question in his eyes.

You just asked my dad! He's not chopped liver.
He can at least teach you the basics.
You change your mind?

Nope. You got your teacher, I got mine.
It's all good.

First Drum Lesson

with Papa Zee and I'm
trying to keep my hands
from shaking.

At least Zee isn't home.
It's still the first week,
and he's already started
private lessons after school.

The drums rest on a rubber mat,
making it possible to move the
entire kit at once.

Papa Zee wipes the dust away
with a wrinkled shirt, a shiny blue
drum set now in the middle of the
living room floor.

Haven't played these things in years.
Reminds me too much of the early days with
Zee's mama, but couldn't bring myself to throw them away.
Now, let's see what we're working with.

He rubs his hand across the taut skins
of the drums, then makes a motion for
me to sit and settle in.

I ease onto the small stool, feeling
nervous still, but special too to have
this alone time with Papa Zee.

It doesn't happen often.

I pour what little I learned from each lesson
into the drums, hitting each piece like a
tornado spiraling out of control.

Papa Zee gently takes the sticks
from my hands, laughing.

That's good. I like your enthusiasm.
Let me show you a few things.

He motions for me to get up, we trade places,
and I take a seat on the sofa, defeated.

Papa Zee settles into a simple beat
with the snare, bass, and cymbal.

Rat-a-tat, rat-a-tat, boom, crash,
rat-a-tat, rat-a-tat, boom, crash.

I tap along on my thigh,
keeping pace with his rhythm.

The more you play, the more you'll develop your ear.
Playing the drums is about control, finesse, style.
Staying in time with the rest of the band.
You can't play louder than your bandmates.
That's never good.

Right now I have one style: loud.

Papa Zee invites me back to the seat,
and I try to replicate what he played,
make it sound like a simple rock beat
the way he did.

Easy, soft, measured, I follow the
pattern he played.

Be patient, April. You'll get there.

I wish someone had taken the time
like this to show me the ropes.
I learned about your age in
New Orleans.

I hear a key in the door and my heart sinks.
Zee comes in making a racket, throwing
his backpack down, kicking off his shoes.

He plods to the kitchen to look inside
the fridge for a snack.

*Would have been home earlier but I found out
one student will get to play a solo at the winter
assembly. Bet it's going to be me once I figure
out what to play to knock their socks off.*

Zee's face lights up when he sees me
behind the drums.

Sorry to interrupt. Keep playing!

Zee plops down on the sofa to watch,
Papa Zee joins him, and both cheer me
on as I try to perfect the pattern I started
before Zee arrived.

After ten minutes, my arms ache.

*This is a good start, April.
Just the beginning,* Papa Zee says.
You're welcome to practice anytime you like.

He follows Zee into the kitchen, the two
suddenly lost in their own company.

Now that Zee's home,
I slide the drums back into
the corner, already thinking
about the next time.

I Skip

across the hall, scream
into the first pillow I see
on the sofa, letting all my
excitement out even though
I'm home alone.

It's happening, at last.

I find a recipe for hot cross buns on
the fridge, the dough still rising
on the counter, my dinner warm
in the microwave.

Mama works the ten-to-six shift,
but the note on my bedroom door
tells me she's gone to the driving range.

Mama hits golf balls when something
is weighing on her that she doesn't
have the words to explain.

She says it's a healthy outlet for
stress, better than some other things
people use to numb their feelings.

While I eat, I watch a drumming video on my
mini iPad and try to follow along with

my sticks on the kitchen table, but
it's not the same. Not at all.

Dinner done, dishes loaded, and before
too long Mama arrives home with her single
club, a big-headed driver she calls Bertha.

Everything good? she asks, slipping
off her sneakers at the door, placing
the golf club in the umbrella stand.

Better than good. Had my first lesson today.

And that went . . .

I tap out a beat on the table.
She gives me a thumbs-up.

Hard day for you? I nod at the club.

Not really. Blowing off some steam.
I want to talk to you about something
after we finish, okay?

The answer is always yes when Mama
lets me bake with her. I dip my finger into
the sweet orange icing while she isn't looking,
then fill the piping bag.

She places twelve rolls on a baking
sheet, and when they are done an
hour later, I make perfect crosses with
the icing.

We devour three buns each,
store the others for breakfast
in the morning.

I'm now full and sleepy.

I start my homework,
she prepares for work.

Zee starts practicing what
sounds like his C major scale.

When my eyes get too heavy,
I kiss Mama good night, cross
the hall to settle on the sofa,
remembering too late that Mama
had something she wanted to talk about.

Practicing Drums

means everyone wears
earplugs, even Mama when
she stops in to check on me,
then darts back across the hall
to her layer of quiet.

Life carries on around me:
Papa Zee calls out new
patterns from the sofa,
clapping on the beat.
Zee in his room working
out a new piece, the notes
unfamiliar, but the sound of
violin strings a welcome
reminder that we're both
making music now.

I beat out the rhythm I know,
rat-a-tat, rat-a-tat, boom, crash,
rat-a-tat, rat-a-tat, boom, boom,
crash. Boom-boom, crash.
And a little hi-hat—
tss-boom-tss-boom-tss—
because I like to experiment.

Lesson Number Two

starts with Papa Zee disappearing
into his bedroom, returning with a
stack of ancient *Drum!* magazines,
some older than me.

I flip through the pages,
thank him, set them aside
on the sofa to pull out the drums.

I learn more about counting.
Music is divided into measures.
Measures divided into notes.
Quarter notes are always four.
This is how to count like a drummer.

Papa Zee keeps time with his
hands—one, two, three, four—
and calls out what I should
play with each beat.

I start to find the rhythm on my own.
My heart feels so full and happy,
like I'm floating, losing myself
in the moment.

I let it rip with a drum roll so fierce,
batabatabatabatabatabatabatbatabat,
that Papa Zee steps back, smiling.

I Remember
to scoop up the magazines
as I retreat to my orderly
apartment.

Welcome home, Mama calls from her bedroom.
There's takeout in the fridge.

I choose three spring rolls,
a helping of chicken pad Thai,
a spoonful of mango sticky rice.

In my bedroom I flip through the
magazine pages, ignore the ads
and interviews with male drummers
until I find one about Sheila E.,
one of the fiercest female drummers
in the world.

I tear the photo out, careful not to rip
the thin page, and tape it to my wall
above my bed.

School Days

feel extra-long this year,
when all I think about is
playing the drums.

Between classes and during lunch
I hide out in the library watching
YouTube video clips of past concerts
at the Boston Garden.

I watch the drummers onstage,
study their beats and patterns,
their hands like hummingbirds,
always in motion.

Wherever I go, Asa is never far.

She settles at the computer
next to mine, looking up scout
activities.

It's always a thrill when I see
a woman on drums, no matter
what band she's playing with,
as long as I can pretend it's me.

The More I Learn

about the drums, the more
time I spend at Zee's apartment.
Between my lessons, practice
sessions, and his new school,
it's impossible not to notice
I'm here more than him.

After dinner and homework,
while he's polishing his violin,
I speak up.

You haven't been home as much.

He flips the violin over to wipe
away every smudge so it looks
like new each time he plays it.

I told Mr. Sanderson about your lessons with my dad.
So I got permission to spend more time practicing at school.
That way we both get better, right?

Thanks, Zee. You pick a song for your solo yet?

Yup, something wicked hard.

Why am I not surprised? I ask.

I scramble off the bed and motion
for him to follow me. Mama left early
for work tonight, but it's after 10:00 p.m.
and time for bed.

He puts his violin into its soft gray case,
zips it closed for the night, and places it on
a messy shelf filled with sheet music.

I wash my face, dry it, slip on my hair bonnet.

Are you going to tell me what it is? I ask from the bathroom.

I *don't want to jinx it.*

In the living room I fluff up my pillow,
smooth out my favorite blanket, plop
down on the sofa.

It's going to be really good, isn't it?

It's gonna make them go crazy!
Night, April.

He turns off the lights in the
living room, eases into his bedroom,
closes the door, and long before I'm asleep,
he's snoring.

The Leaves Start

changing, deep greens
now red, yellow, and orange.

I hustle home from school
each day to practice,
drumming out the patterns
I learn during my weekly
lessons.

Papa Zee knows the drill by now.
When I arrive home, he's already
pulled the drums onto the floor,
put in his earplugs.

I start off the way I usually do,
warming up my arms and legs
by hitting my sticks together,
the clack-clack-clack-clack
and boom-boom-boom-boom
from hitting the bass drum pedal
vibrating through my whole body.

Sometimes Papa Zee comes out
of his room to watch, and even with
an audience of one, I put on a show.

Dom dom-bam, dom dom-bam,
dom dom-bam, tss, tss-tss.

I love the sounds of the hi-hat
and bass drum the most, one
high and sweet, the other
loud and deep.

Each combination I play
from memory sounds more
like a drummer, more like
I'm making music.

Making the Most

of my playing time after
school because Zee also
has lessons now on Mondays.

It's getting darker earlier,
and today was wet and
gray. I can still hear the rain
pelting on the window in
Zee's bedroom.

There's nothing I like more
than getting into a rhythm,
playing loud and loose, but
today I choose a simple
drum roll, trying to match
the sounds of the rain.

I let my hands move faster,
rocking a triple-beat drum roll,
sweat beading on my forehead.
On the edge of my seat, I'm in the zone,
the feeling I love most when
playing the drums.

An Hour Passes

and I've worked up
an appetite. Papa Zee
waves me over to the table
for an extra-large slice of key
lime pie, another reason I
love Papa Zee.

Got a good one for you.
What makes songs but never sings?

I dig into the pie, shrug my shoulders.

Notes! You should write these down, April.
Never know when a good joke will come in handy.
Want whipped cream?

Papa Zee limps to the
kitchen, his ankle injury flaring
up again. Two years ago a
dog bit him on his postal route:
seven stitches, a week at home.

Hazard of the job, he'd said.

A job I know because last year
we convinced Mama to let me

skip school so I could shadow
him while he delivered mail for
Take Your Daughter to Work Day.

It's one of my favorite memories
with Papa Zee, walking the streets,
waving at the women flirting with him,
blushing when I ran up the stairs to
hand someone their mail, him all smiles,
bad jokes, telling people,

Better watch out! This girl is going places!

Me carrying my sticks,
making beats in the air.

Back from the kitchen, he shakes
the can, makes a crooked smiley
face on my slice of pie.

You're making great progress. You're a natural, you know? he asks.

I dig into my pie, chew quickly,
swallow before I reply.

Think I'm good enough yet to convince Mama to get me some drums?

Papa Zee laughs so hard he starts choking.
I drop my fork, push away my plate.
That wasn't the response I was expecting.

When he catches his breath, he cuffs
me by the neck, plants a kiss on my head.
Don't get mad. I'm not laughing at you, April.
It's not how well you play. It's the instrument you play.
Maybe Chantelle will come around.
But a woman who likes quiet as much as your mama does . . .

Humph.

I finish the last few bites of my pie,
take our dishes to the kitchen sink.

Shouldn't Zee be home by now?

Papa Zee shifts back in his seat,
fingers laced across his belly,
calm.

His teacher promised to bring him home after the lesson.
He's working hard for this solo. It means so much to him.

Sometimes I listen for a clue to what song
he's chosen for his solo, but so far nothing.
He's being super secretive, which is a first.

Zee walks through the door, shaking off the rain.
From the short walk from the car to the building
he's drenched, but his violin case is safe in a large
plastic garbage bag.

Not taking any chances with this. Not now.

A crack of thunder makes us all jump.

Not even a hint about your solo? I tease.

Zee smirks as a response and starts stripping
out of his wet clothes and shoes, leaving them
by the door.

Lucky for you I'm patient! See you later.

I give Papa Zee a quick hug, Zee a shoulder shove.
I'm out the door and across the hall when I
notice a crack in one of my sticks.

Class Project #2:

an art project, drawing
a profile portrait of your
partner. Asa and me again.

Most of the morning Asa
nods off during the lesson.
I poke her whenever Ms.
Chisholm looks our way.

She napped through lunch, and
now that we're working in pairs
I notice her stomach is louder
than her voice.

Even though we can't eat or
chew gum in class, I slip her
a mini Snickers bar.

She chews with her mouth
open, smacks like it's the
best piece of candy she's
ever had.

Ms. Chisholm gives us both
the stink eye. Asa swallows
fast.

Thanks, Asa says. *Mom forgot to pack my lunch.*

Wanna hear some good news? She quickly changes the subject.
I got my Drawing badge two summers ago.
You any good at drawing, April?

She fidgets in her bag for a lime-green
sash covered in colorful round patches.

No, I can't draw. Not even a straight line with a ruler.

Asa stifles a laugh, but at least
her stomach stops growling.

Besides lunch, Asa could also use more sleep,
but I guess one day isn't a big deal.

She's off to the supply closet, and I'm
dreaming up beats in my head, tapping
them out on my desk until I get the
look again from Ms. Chisholm telling
me now is not the time or place.

Asa returns with paper and charcoal
pencils and gets right to work, which is
so Asa.

She captures my button nose, ponytail,
and almond-shaped eyes much better than
I expected. I stop her when she pulls out

a chestnut-brown pencil to shade it in, shaking
my head *don't.*

My skin is more like cinnamon, my hair
wavy in my ponytail, and I don't want her
to change a thing about the picture.

My turn. I make her eyes too big,
nose too small, her ear barely visible
against the beige construction paper.

That's okay. You tried. I like watercolor better.

As students walk their creations
to the board to share, I remember Asa
had one scout badge she wanted
to get before the end of the year.

I ask her about it.

It's my Junior First Aid badge.

Asa perks up, offers her
best smile. I smile too.

Hope you get it, I say, meaning it.

Me too.

Might Be Time

to see what all the fuss is
about this new school where
Zee spends so much time.

I go in search of Zee, hoping
I'll surprise him, maybe even
hear a sneak peek of his solo.

The hallways are empty, but I
hear music from a classroom
nearby.

I whiz through the colorful
hallways with the cool murals
of famous people:

Mae Jemison.
Misty Copeland.
George Washington Carver.
Marian Anderson.
Questlove.

Looking for the room where
cymbals crash, a bass drum
thumps, I find a red-haired boy
with freckles and his teacher.

The boy stops when I appear in
the doorway. The teacher turns
in my direction.

May I help you?

He's tall, skinny, and wears a
three-piece suit with thick
black-framed glasses too
big for his face.

I play drums too.

The boy starts kicking the bass
drum on the two-and-four beats
impatiently.

The teacher sighs, pointing to
my uniform that is most definitely
not navy blue and khaki.

What is your name?

The way he says it sounds
like I'm in trouble. I back away,
prepared to sprint, but when I hear my
name echoing through the hall, I freeze in place.

April? April! What are you doing here? Zee says.

When Zee reaches us, the teacher's
face brightens, his whole body shifts.
He tells the student to keep practicing
and excuses himself.

Mr. Sanderson, this is April. My best friend.
The one taking drum lessons? She's pretty good too.
But we have to get home. Sorry to bother you, Jacob.

Zee waves to the kid on drums and
tugs me toward the front door, like
the school is on fire.

I Almost Missed

you, Zee says as he
marches across the street,
turning toward home.

I *left something in my locker. Had to go back to get it since . . .*
I *won't be in school tomorrow.*

I ease my walk to a crawl,
making him slow down too.

Hold up. Is tomorrow a holiday? I ask.
I *have school tomorrow.*

Not a holiday. I *fainted while* I *was practicing my solo.*
The school nurse called Daddy.

I pull Zee's arm to make him stop.

Is *that why you were rushing us out?*
You okay now? That must have been scary.

It was only, like, thirty seconds. No big deal.
Probably didn't eat enough breakfast.
I *can't play at school again until* I *get a doctor's note.*

When we reach the apartment lobby,
it smells like Lysol, and we both cover

our noses with our jackets until we get
into the elevator.

I glance at Zee while we're riding to
our floor. Him fainting is something
that never happened before.

My Apartment Is Empty

and it's family night. I change
out of my uniform into jeans and
a sweatshirt, take my drumsticks
to Papa Zee's like always.

Can't really play with one cracked
stick, but it's comforting to carry
them anyway.

I think about Zee again, his
fainting at his new school,
not wanting to tell me about
his solo when we used to tell
each other everything.

I love taking lessons, trying
new patterns even if they don't
always sound right at first.
Zee is changing, but so am I.

Before I Open

the door across
the hall, I hear old-school
rap and laughter.

When I step inside,
things are in full swing,
and there's a woman
with platinum-blond braids
down her back I've never
seen before, mid-story.

What clubs have you played in the city? she asks Papa Zee.

*The Red Room, Paradise Rock, Howl at the Moon,
Royale,* Papa Zee says, rattling off the names,

and then they say in unison . . . *Wally's Cafe.*

They both laugh like old friends
meeting again after too long.

Zee waves me inside,
his eyes big, smile gone.

A moment ago he looked
like he was enjoying the

stranger's company, hanging
on her every word.

Mama springs to her feet,
looking guilty.

April, this is Robin. She's joining us for dinner.
We were waiting on you to arrive before we started.

That's pretty obvious.
Everyone is hunkered around
the table with plates of pizza.

I mumble a pathetic hello and look to Zee
for a clue about this stranger,
but he's distracted by picking
the mushrooms off his slice.

The laughter and easy conversation
that greeted me when I arrived fades
into a hushed silence. But not for long.

The woman Mama invited is pretty,
pecan brown, full bodied, with a small
gap between her front teeth.

She talks so fast it's like she's afraid
if she took a breath, she'd forget what
she wanted to say.

Nice to finally meet you, April.
I've heard so much about you.
You should know I don't believe in woo-woo stuff.
Meeting Chantelle felt like fate.
I noticed her during shift changes at work.
Finally got up the nerve to introduce myself.

Mama must think this woman is special.
She's never invited anyone to family night.

This must have been what Mama
wanted to talk about after we baked
the hot cross buns.

Zee catches my eye, shrugs his shoulders,
telling me he didn't know either. When I look
at Papa Zee, he looks away, fast.

I can only imagine what you're thinking, the woman says.

Hmmm, I say.

This new woman is waiting for me to say . . . what?

The apartment feels like it's shrinking.
I head to the kitchen to load my plate
with slices of pepperoni, one veggie,
and choose to sit on the sofa to eat.

But I've lost my appetite.

She Won't Quit

talking, even when it's clear
I'm not interested in what
she has to say.

First time Mama brings a date home,
and I can't believe this is how I meet her.

Zander was telling us what a quick learner you are.
Drums, right? I'd love to see you play sometime.

When I don't reply, she moves on.

And, Zee, you play violin? Me too.

Zee perks up, looking like he can't
wait to tell her his entire playing history,
but I give him the look that says this is not cool.

Yeah, that's right. We both play music, he says.

Another awkward silence.

Papa Zee clears his throat.

Robin here didn't come empty-handed. She brought dessert.
Don't know about you all, but I never turn down a slice of apple pie,
especially when there's ice cream.

Even though I want to be mad at him
for not warning me, I guess
it wasn't his business to tell.

Robin whips out a pie from a bag
on the chair next to her.

It's from one of the best bakeries in the city.
Hope you all like it. It's my favorite.

Papa Zee grabs the ice cream,
Zee snags the bowls from the
cabinet.

Mama's staring at her hands,
the walls, everywhere but at me.

I may be able to give Papa Zee
a pass, but Mama?

If she thinks getting this woman to
ask about my drumming and
offer to watch me play is going to
be enough for me to like her, she's
dead wrong.

Not Today,

not tomorrow, likely not ever
will I like this woman with the big
brown eyes, long pretty lashes
who has shown up in my life
without warning.

Why didn't you tell me she was coming?

Our apartment is extra quiet
as Mama puts away a single
slice of that nasty pie that I
won't eat. Even if it was good,
I wouldn't have liked it because
I never like fruit in my dessert.

The least Mama could have done
is told that woman that she should
have picked something else.

*I thought it would be easier to
introduce her to everyone at once.
So you wouldn't feel singled out.*

She's right that I would have liked
tonight a thousand times less if it
had been only the three of us, but Mama
still should have tried harder to tell me first.

Between Zee fainting and this
stranger showing up, all I want
to do is bury my head beneath
my pillow.

I start my bedtime routine,
savoring the quiet for once.
As I'm adding a second
drummer to my wall—this
time Cindy Blackman, who
plays with Lenny Kravitz—
Mama appears in my doorway.

I'm sorry. It wasn't the best first impression.
She's kind and funny and good company.
I think you'll like her if you give her a chance.

I give my two posters a high five
and plop down on my bed, pull
the covers over my head.

I doubt it. Good night.

First Thing

the next morning, Papa Zee
whisks Zee off to the doctor.

I race home from school
nervous about my friend,
distracted all day long,
impatient to hear the news.

I find Zee stomping about
the apartment, picking up things,
putting them down, not sure
what to do with his hands.

Zander Jr., it's just for a little while. I promise.
A few days off from playing won't hurt you.

It's like I'm a fly on the wall.
That never feels good when
they're having an argument.

Papa Zee almost never calls Zee by
his given name, much less throw in Junior.

The doctor says I'm okay, Dad. Remember?
We were both there. I heard him with my own ears.
Jonathon at school faints every time he sees blood.

Hello? I'm here, I interrupt.
What's going on?

Fainting at the sight of blood isn't the same thing.
You were in the middle of physical activity when you fainted.
The doctor said you could be pushing yourself too hard.

So what if I am? What's the worst that's going to happen?
I'll get the solo? Maybe get a scholarship to Berklee or Juilliard?

Papa Zee's posture softens,
his shoulders slump. He looks
like a balloon that's lost its air.

I hear you, Zee. I do. But hear me out.
When I was a sophomore in high school,
we had a wide receiver on the football team
who was fast as lightning, had hands that
could catch impossible passes. College scouts
from everywhere were calling him.

Zee starts pacing the room,
impatient. I plop down on the sofa,
unsure what's the point of this story.

One day in practice he was running a play.
The quarterback threw it long and he jumped

high in the air to catch it. He caught it all right.
But he came crashing to the ground.
And he stayed there.

Boy wasn't even sixteen yet. Sudden cardiac arrest.
So much promise. Gone.

Zee stops pacing, looks at his
dad with a scowl.

I don't play football. Never have.
And don't plan on starting.

It's not just about football, Zee.
Don't you see what I'm saying?

Yeah. Something was wrong with that kid.
Dad, stop being weird. Doctor said I was fine.

Zee sulks to his bedroom.

I follow but settle at his desk,
giving him space because he's
still so mad I can see his nostrils
flaring.

I Try

to lighten the mood
by changing the subject,
getting his mind off the
fight.

That was weird, right? And last night was weirder.
What did you think of that woman who came to dinner?

Zee plucks a stress ball that
looks like a mini-basketball
from his nightstand, not that
he'd ever play a sport for real.

In the time since school started,
Zee grew another inch, his hair
grew three. He's sporting a short
afro and changing before my eyes.

She was all right. I liked her.
She and Dad got along great.
Your mom was super nervous!

She should have been!

We take turns shooting at
the small basketball hoop
at the top of his closet door.

He looks more relaxed, and
it might be a risk to upset him
again, but I'm dying to know.

What did the doctor say?

He didn't tell me to stop playing. He listened to my heart.
Asked a bunch of questions about family history and stuff.
It's not like I can ask my mother.

Zee's mom was a woman with
music in her bones who went
searching for a melody, a song
only she could hear, and never
returned.

And you're feeling okay?

Better than okay. It was one stupid time I fainted!

He springs from the bed
to make a slam dunk
on the closet door hoop,
looking as healthy and full of energy
as always.

That's good enough for me.

Twenty-Four Hours

later I discover Zee in the basement
of the building, hiding in the
janitor's closet in an empty
laundry room, practicing his
violin when he's supposed to
be resting.

It's Thursday, and if his playing
wasn't on pause, he'd be at
his private lessons after school.

Don't tell, okay? Dad would have a fit.

I load the whites, then the colors,
watch the clothes start to spin,
the suds rise.

Was that your solo? I ask, trying to remember the melody.

Nope, just scales. Don't want to get rusty.

I sit cross-legged on the floor next to him,
start tapping out a beat, and he joins in with
a melody to complement what I do.

Badadadadada, boop, boop, bap,
badadadadada, boop, boop, bap.

We're really getting into it when another
resident arrives to remove his clothes
from the dryer. He smiles at us,
gives us a thumbs-up when he leaves.

Where does Papa Zee think you are?

In my room resting. I asked him not to disturb me.
I closed the door and snuck out while he was in the bathroom.
What about you? Why aren't you practicing?

I tell him about my cracked drumstick,
my plan to ask Mama to take me to the
music store on Mass Ave. to get new ones.

Robin plays the drums too. Maybe that's a good sign.
Your mama can't hate on the drums forever.
Or can she?

Stop it! I punch him in the arm.
You got out of the house, but you'll need to get back in.
I can distract Papa Zee while you slip back into your bedroom.

You'd do that for me? he asks playfully.

What else is a best friend for?

Word.

I Dig Out

my winter coat and hat
from my closet, the late
October air crisp
today.

It wasn't so long ago that the
leaves were starting to change
and now most have fallen.

There's a store on Mass Ave.
where we're going to buy my
new drumsticks. I would've invited Zee,
but he's finally back to practicing,
and things are less tense between
him and Papa Zee.

Driving to the store, Mama's
not one for small talk. It's been
five days since she brought Robin
to family dinner and I'm still mad.

How are things going with the drums?

Her asking about the drums
is like a polar bear asking to
visit Miami, but at least she's
taking me to the music store.

Haven't been able to play all week.
It'll be better when I have new sticks.

I'm sure Mama wants to talk to me
about Robin. It's bad enough since
they started dating Mama isn't home
as much, ordering more takeout,
warming up more leftovers.

I am curious about Robin
and her playing music, but I
refuse to give Mama the wrong idea.

I haven't forgotten family night
and won't forgive that easily.

The store is bigger than it looks
from the outside, packed with
music books, sheet music,
and instruments.

The practice drums are in
a soundproof glass room.
I pick a pair of Vic Firth 5A hickory,
tear-drop tips that I found
in *Drum!* magazine, test them,
and get carried away in the moment.

Even though Mama can't hear me,
she taps on the glass for me to stop.

At the register, something else
catches my eye. A gift for Zee.
A digital metronome, even though
Christmas is more than a month
away. Mama happily buys it.

Across the street I watch as
Berklee students move about with
instruments big and small.

One day, maybe, that'll be me.

Weird Times

at school and home,
Asa's desk empty for
two straight days and
Zee so focused on his
solo that he practices
every waking moment.

When Asa returns, her
head is heavy again.
Staying awake seems
like a chore she can't be
bothered to do.

You been camping in your backyard or something? I say,
keeping the mood light.

Asa's hazel eyes water, and she
excuses herself from class, spending
the rest of the day in the nurse's office.

Weirdest start to a week ever.

I'm So Happy

each time I take my seat behind
the drums with my new sticks.

I'm setting up my stool to begin
when Zee arrives from his private
lesson early, his coat flapping open,
hat thrown on the sofa, smile wide.

I *got the solo!*

He jumps around the living room
and I join him. Not even two months
since he started at the new school
and he's already showing out.
He bangs on Papa Zee's closed door
to tell him too.

Papa Zee appears from his room,
hugs Zee so big, he swallows up
his whole body like he used to
when Zee was younger.

Let's play together, April!
I'll play, then you play, just like . . .

He catches himself before spilling
the beans about the laundry room.

Like a call-and-response, I chime in.

Let's do it.

Zee removes his violin from
the soft gray case, tunes his
strings, and I start tapping my
foot on a four count.

He starts playing one of his favorites,
"When the Saints Go Marching In,"
because Papa Zee loves it too,
being from New Orleans.

When Zee pauses, I slide
in with the thump of bass
and a run of rat-a-tat-tats on
the snare, and we do that
back and forth, him swaying
as he plays, my heart soaring,
hands working, brain buzzing
from the adrenaline until I bring
us to a close with a cymbal CRASH!

The Next Morning

as soon as we hit the sidewalk
to begin our walk to school,
I have an idea.

We should totally start a band!
We could play like we did last night.

The twin apartment towers
grow smaller behind us as
we walk, their shadows
stretched like a two-finger
peace sign on the pavement
beneath the barren trees.

After playing together last night,
I'm convinced we can play in
a city park, maybe even in front
of Berklee.

It's a little unusual, don't you think?
A drum-and-violin duo? But maybe . . .

I can't think of another one either,
but that doesn't mean it can't exist.
I change the subject.

Guess who's coming to Thanksgiving?

Zee shrugs.

That woman. At least Mama told me this time.

She has a name. It's Robin.
Maybe this time you'll be nicer to her.

Zee shifts his backpack,
bends to wipe two specks
of dust from his loafers.

Maybe she won't talk so much.

We're nearing the corner
in no time, no more strolling
down the street like on warmer
days.

Wanna hear Daddy's latest joke?
Why don't we watch the symphony on TV?
Because of all the violins!

Ha! I get it. It's a play on violence.

Zee raises his hand for a high five
and I don't leave him hanging.

And it made you smile.

Class Project #3:
starts off Thanksgiving week,
a poetry project this time.

Asa is a no-show again.

I get paired with the twins.
Each group receives
a single page from the local
newspaper and takes turns
choosing words to
black out to create a poem.

Even though I'm a third wheel,
the twins let me start with the
first paragraph while they debate
the rest of the words to black out,
which to keep.

I complete my part of the project
with plenty of class time to spare.

It's an article about a local college
student who travels abroad to learn
a new language.

I black out so many words, but I'm
happy with what's left:

Exhaling,
we take our chances,
we thrive anyway.

I wonder what's going on
with Asa. Her attendance is as
sparse as my black-out poem.
Can't imagine how she gets
away with missing so much
school.

Thanksgiving Eve,

while Mama's at work,
Papa Zee is in his room,
Zee and I do our homework together.

Popcorn is our favorite study food.
We play with our food by blurting out,
Incoming! and throwing a kernel
in the other's direction to see
if they can catch it in their mouth.

Keeps homework more interesting.

Incoming! I say, throwing a piece Zee's way.

Zee is pitched forward on his bed,
like someone sucker punched him.

Zee? You okay?

I throw a second kernel at his
head just in case he's being
silly, but my gut already tells
me something is wrong.

I shove his arm gently until his
head slowly rises.

What's going on, Zee? Are you fainting again?

I sit next to him on the bed. He still doesn't talk.

Is this what happened to you at school?

He takes a deep breath, sits up straight,
devours the popcorn I threw at him.

Not fainting. More like heart racing.

I'm two steps toward the door,
about to tell Papa Zee.

No! he says, whispering loudly.
Please. Don't tell Dad.

Only if you tell me what's going on.

I *don't know what it is. It's only happened twice.*
The first day of school. And today.
I *take deep breaths until my heart slows down again.*
Problem solved.

I think about what he's saying,
remember that moment in the
hallway that morning,
but it still doesn't feel right.

What happens if your deep breaths don't help?

I study his eyes, hoping for a sign.

Zee grabs a handful of popcorn,
throws a few kernels in the air,
catches all five in his mouth.

If it happens again, I'll tell Daddy.
I've got less than three weeks to my solo.
Promise you won't say anything?
Not even to your mom. Promise?

My worry is hard to swallow,
like a piece of stale bread
caught in my throat.

Promise.

Thanksgiving Day
is always a big affair for the
Ellis-Jackson family.

We start the day at the local
food pantry feeding others who
don't have what we do.

At home, Papa Zee sets the Cajun
turkey baking, Mama lets the monkey
bread rise. There's twice as much
food as there are people, including
when Robin shows up with a red
velvet cake this time.

This looks delicious, Papa Zee says,
walking the cake to the kitchen.

I see him swipe a small bit of frosting from the side,
and he laughs when he notices I've seen him.

He's wearing a black-and-gold-plaid sweater, black
slacks, this being one of the few days each year
he dresses up. We all look good, though.

If it weren't Turkey Day, I'd suggest we start with dessert.
I expect that won't fly with Chantelle, right?

Mama smiles, relaxes her shoulders.
Her silver-streaked locs are freshly twisted,
framing her round face like a perfect halo.

I'll never say so, but her and Robin,
who wears a deep orange V-neck dress
with calf-high brown leather boots,
make a cute couple.

Thank you for allowing me to join you, Robin says.

We're happy you came. Aren't we?
Zee kicks me under the table.

I kick him back, still smiling at everyone else.

Happy is *not* the word I would use.
More like *tolerating her presence.*
I'm guessing Mama hopes Robin
might be sticking around.

I'd rather she not.

Can't remember the last time Mama baked
anything other than the bread for tonight's
dinner. Is this what it's like to date someone?
You stop doing all the things you used to do?

No thanks.

We haven't talked about Robin much since
that first visit. It's been almost a month, and
every time Mama brings her up,
I change the subject.

Between bites of food, I ignore everybody
else and watch Zee closely, waiting for the
moment when he pitches forward again.
It never comes.

Mama clears her throat, gives me
the *look* that says I should pay
more attention to Robin.

Do you have kids? I ask.

Robin perks up.

I don't, but I love kids.
I have eight nieces and nephews.

Then why aren't you spending the holiday with them?

April Janelle Jackson!

I know I'm pressing my luck.
Mama has but so much patience.

It's okay, Chantelle. That's a great question.
I spend a lot of time with my family.
I coach my nieces' basketball team in the winter.
And my nephews' Little League baseball team.
Today they are with family members who don't live local.
Not to worry, we all spend Christmas together.

I wasn't expecting that answer, but at least
now I know she won't be here on Christmas.

Thanks, I say quietly.

Well, now that we got all that out of the way . . . Papa Zee says,
I've got a good one to share.

Everyone but Robin says *nooo,*
and Papa Zee fakes hurt feelings.

Fine, then it's time for dessert.

Ever Since

that night Zee told me
about his racing heart,
I can't stop thinking about it.

Can't stop wondering if, like
his escape to the laundry room,
he's bending the truth or just
stubborn. It's been two weeks,
and all signs point to him being
okay, so maybe it's nothing.

The days are shorter,
the weather much colder.

I never liked winter.
The only thing that helped
was having Zee in class,
us entertaining each other
to pass the time.

I feel like I'm not ready
for this next season.

Zee spends all his time
at school now, and I see
Mama some nights for an
hour after she comes home

from hanging out with Robin,
and then she's gone to work.

Guess that's easier for her
to do when she knows
I can grab my stuff, cross
the hall, and stay the night at Zee's.

I practice three times as often
as I have lessons, and tonight
I warn Papa Zee to put in his
earplugs because I'm about to
light up the kit.

I'm a one-girl band,
shifting from an 8th-note groove,
a little bass, snare, hi-hat to the
shuffle groove, adding in a cymbal,
and testing all my skills as I work up
to the 16th-note groove.

Ninety minutes later I've lost all my steam.

Papa Zee comes out of his room clapping.

You're developing your stamina.
And getting better by the week.

I wipe the sweat from my brow.

Wondering if maybe you're ready for the next level.

You mean like a new teacher?

Wouldn't be the worst thing for you.

The thought brings back my earlier
lessons and I shudder. I change the subject.

You getting ready for the season? I ask.

I nod in the direction of the Santa Claus
costume hanging on his bedroom door,
still in the plastic from the dry cleaners.

You know it. Haven't missed a Christmas yet.
What about you?

I'm excited about Zee's present that I got him.
And his solo. You know what he's playing?

Well . . . , Papa Zee hedges. I've heard a few things.
Won't be long now before you'll both show off
your skills during family night.
Zee's not the only musician in the family.

I skip around the house,
bursting with anticipation.

Right!

I push the drums back into
their corner, thrilled by the
idea that Zee and me get to
put on our first family show.

The First Snow Falls

as I arrive home after school,
flakes big as cotton balls.

I know they won't stick, too big
and wet to make tomorrow the
first snow day of the year.

Only three more days before
winter recess, less than
twenty-four hours before Zee's
solo.

I add two new pictures
to my bedroom wall—Nikki Glaspie
and Terri Lyne Carrington—
grateful as ever for
the company.

I love my collection
of Drum Mavens.

Solo Day . . . Finally,

and Zee waits in the hallway
dressed in a black tuxedo,
red-sequin bow tie, the sharpest-
looking eleven-year-old in Boston.

It's weird not seeing him in his
uniform, but he got special permission.

Papa Zee, late as usual,
rushes toward the elevator
but stops cold to tell Zee
exactly what we all know:

You're going to play the roof off that place.
You sure you don't want me to come to school today?
I'd happily listen to you play it again tonight.

Zee reaches out to Papa Zee and hugs him quick.
Dad! I want everyone to hear it together.
Papa Zee shrugs, waves as he walks backward to the
elevator, leaving us behind like it's any other school day.

On the Way to School,

Zee bounces down the street
already hearing the applause,
like the sidewalk is his red carpet.

I can sneak out and come see you.
Maybe hover in a corner out of sight?

We're three blocks from the
intersection where we'll part
ways, and he reaches for my
hand, squeezes.

It's the first solo. Won't be my last.
I go on at 12:05. I'm so ready.
Do not worry. Okay? I feel fine.

I am worried. What if he faints again?
I don't hug him. I don't want to wrinkle
his clothes and instead straighten his bow tie,
giving my best smile.

At the intersection he's off running,
waving, screaming goodbye
into the wind.

When the Clock Strikes

noon, I scramble to find
a corner of the playground
all to myself, bundled up
to keep warm.

Five blocks apart feels
like miles away, and I wait
until exactly 12:05 p.m., when
I squeeze my eyes closed
so tight that tears build
behind my lids.

I can see him in my mind's eye,
standing tall, fingers moving
across the strings, biting into the
flesh of his fingertips.

I strain to hear those first notes of
a song I won't know until tonight,
my body bouncing, my fingers
tapping out a beat on my
thigh before my concentration
is shattered.

What are you doing, April?
Are you crying?

When I open my eyes,
Asa is so close I can see
the flecks of green in hers,
and I back into the fence.

Not right now, Asa. Please.

Asa eases away, her face
crumpled in hurt.

I came late today.
Just wanted you to know I'm back.

I close my eyes again, the feeling
lost with two hours and forty-five
minutes left of this school day,
and that feels way too long.

The Last Bell

rings and I break out of my
classroom, down the hallway
through the front doors, and
don't stop until I'm at the
intersection.

Zee's already there with
Mr. Sanderson, who wears
a black suit, a shiny black shirt,
and a red pocket square.

He's got his hand on Zee's shoulder,
both beaming.

You should be very proud of Zander.
His performance was flawless.
One of the best I've heard in years.

Zee looks more relieved than proud,
more proof stacking in his favor that
he's still a star shining so bright it's
like looking into the sun.

I told him you've been making good progress with the drums.
May be time to take your lessons to the next level?

Zee must have been talking to Papa Zee,

but now is not the time to spoil this
good moment.

From what Zander describes you've got a good foundation.
I have some availability for private lessons.
What do you like most about playing the drums?

I like how alive and free and wild
I feel, like I'm playing within time,
but bending it too, but I'm not telling
him any of that.

I'm counting in my head while
Mr. Sanderson waits on my reply.

I'm up to five Mississippis, but
it's clear Zee isn't budging until
I respond.

Thank you. I'll think about it.

I give Zee a look for not warning me
about his plan, but he's still
feeling so good from his solo
to notice.

Besides, I'm too happy for him to be mad.

In the Time

I've been at school,
Mama has pulled out the
tabletop Christmas tree,
decorated it with a string
of white lights.

Three gifts sit beneath the
tree:

one for me,
one for Zee,
one for Mama,
wrapped like Robin
paid good money to
make it perfect.

The double-taped ends mean
no peeking at the gift with the fancy
cursive writing and too-sweet perfume.

Mama's always been light
on words, short on emotion,
and not a fan of most holidays.

Not Valentine's Day,
not Veterans Day,
not even Mother's Day,

and Christmas is always
hit-or-miss.

Sometimes no decorations
at all, but this year there's
Robin and now the tabletop tree.

This Family Night

Papa Zee ordered dinner special from our
favorite soul-food spot. He unpacks collards,
mac and cheese, whipped sweet potatoes,
pulled pork, and ribs, scattering the containers
across the kitchen counter.

We fill our plates buffet-style.

A *standing ovation, huh?* Papa Zee can't help himself.
Tell me again how many people, Zee?

Mama clears the cluttered dining table.

I *told you it was the whole school.*
At least three hundred, maybe more?

Papa Zee turns the volume up on
a Beyoncé song, swinging, dipping,
and turning like he's onstage.

You hear that, Chantelle? April?
How many seats are at Symphony Hall, Zee?

Of course, Zee knows this answer by heart.

There are 2,625 seats during symphony season.
At least that's what the website says.

That's my boy! That's a good start!
Don't y'all think?

Better than good, Mama says.

I agree.

The Last Time

I remember Papa Zee this
excited was the night he streamed
an old NAACP Image Awards show,
introducing us to a colorful man
with a guitar, a striking woman
on the drums.

Zee and me watched that performance
of Prince and Sheila E. every night for a
week, mesmerized, pretending we too
were performing on an awards show in
front of thousands.

In the time that four songs have played,
we've finished dinner. I retrieve my new
sticks and make a special point to hand
out earplugs before putting in my own.

I count myself in with my sticks,
start with a drum roll before breaking
into a slow simple rock beat, the first one
Papa Zee taught me.

A tempo shift and I'm
jamming on a dance beat
so solid—and I know I'm doing
okay because even Mama taps her toe,

Papa Zee snaps his fingers,
looking as proud of me
as he is of Zee.

Zee keeps time with his
bow, waving it about in the air
like a conductor, nodding his head
on every beat in support.

This is just a warm-up for Zee's
big solo, I know, but I'm loving
the chance to show off my skills.

Mama and Papa Zee
clap for me after they remove
their earplugs, and it's the best
feeling in the world.

Zee gives me a double high five
before warming up his strings.

In school, Zee explains,
he learns to play dead
white men

Chopin . . .
Brahms . . .

Mozart ...
Beethoven ...

but for this solo he chose something
he knew no one at his school could
compete with.

We three squeeze into the cracked
leather sofa, and Zee winks at me,
telling me he's ready.

Ladies and gentlemen, tonight I'll be playing
"Let's Go Crazy" by Prince. Settle in.
It's gonna be a good time.

The first measures start slow and quiet,
then the tempo picks up, like a car going
from zero to sixty in no time, Zee moving
the bow so fast over the strings they
start to shred.

Mama and Papa Zee pop up and start dancing together.

I spin and twirl, clap and laugh out
loud because of course Zee would
pick a song this awesome.

Zee puts his all into the song,
sweat streaming down his face,
his body rising up and dipping low
with the melody until the song slows
down again as he nears the end.

Papa Zee whistles,
high-pitched and loud.

Mama keeps dancing,
singing, "*Let's go crazy /*
Let's get nuts."

I give Zee a double high five
and a hug, and we fall
onto the sofa, laughing.

He's right. All those extra lessons,
days spent after school practicing,
totally worth it.

All of it.

More Snow Falls

as I remember the
highlights of the day,
me staring at the photos
of the Drum Mavens on
my wall, wondering again
about my own future.

Should I reconsider lessons
with Mr. Sanderson?

If Zee can learn a song that
hard, play it that well, what
might I be able to do?

It's nice being in my own bed,
having Mama home tonight
after such an extraordinary day.

I do love having two places to
call home, not to mention two
apartments are better than one
when only one of them can house
the drums.

Two More Days

of school, only four days
before I get to give
Zee his Christmas present,
my palms sweat in my mittens,
my body feels electric as we
walk to the intersection.

Wasn't last night amazing? I ask.

Feels like we're walking through a
snow globe, the flakes dancing around
us as we hurry down the street.

Zee seems distracted and he's
walking faster than usual.

You were so nervous at the start of school.
You playing like that? Bet they didn't know what hit them.

I mean it as a joke, but Zee doesn't laugh.
I stop walking. He doesn't. I run to catch up.

You know I worked superhard, right?

My fists are clenched tight
and I shake my fingers free.
I didn't mean to offend him.

I know. Sorry. I know.

Don't mean to snap on you, April.
I'm ready for this holiday break . . .
and my presents.

He nudges me with his elbow, smiling.

The past few months have been a lot.

We nod our heads in unison,
let those words settle in the air
between us until the memories
are too many to consider any longer.

A block before we part, Zee gathers
a handful of snow—hard, icy crystals—
and offers a mischievous smile as he
starts a snowball fight.

I dodge his sad attempt, throw
one back, our first snowball fight
of the season.

No Asa Again

at school, what else is new,
must be traveling already
for the holiday, leaving me
free to think about Zee.

Will he like his present?
Should I have gotten him
something else, like a new
bow tie for his next solo?

Nobody in class is
paying attention and
the hours can't pass
fast enough.

After school, I wait at the
intersection for five minutes,
then ten, as students from
both schools clear out,
tiny flakes still falling like
sugar on the empty streets.

Where is Zee?

No Trace

of Zee's footprints on the
path back to the apartment,
but I walk home convinced
I'll find him waiting for me,
jamming on his violin in his
socks in the living room.

It feels like forever for the
elevator to come.

I huff up the twelve
flights of stairs.

Papa Zee's door is open.

He and Mama stand in the
middle of the living room,
two statues rock-still.

Papa Zee is in his postal blues,
violin case in hand,
tears falling in buckets.

Mama's face is puffy, eyes
swollen almost shut.

Papa Zee? Mama, what's going on?

Papa Zee mutters something about
someone doing their best, but it was
too late.

What are you talking about?
Where is Zee?

Papa Zee looks at me standing
in the doorway, more through
me, not seeing me at all.

He's gone. Zee's gone.

Mama wails like she'd brought Zee
into the world herself, her tears
shocking me into stillness.

I'm too angry to cry, too disappointed
with myself for not speaking up these
past few weeks, for wasting precious time.

Shoulda, Coulda, Woulda

said something, told somebody,
if I hadn't made that stupid promise.

I wasn't braver or smarter,
didn't listen harder to that little
voice inside my head that said
hearts shouldn't beat that way.

I kept his secret like I said
I would, and what good did it
do him?

Do us?

The First Night

without Zee feels like a
bad dream on repeat,
a record scratched and
skipping the same refrain.

Papa Zee all cried out in his room,
me sucking air through my mouth,
rapid blinking at Zee's door, waiting
to see him again.

Not quite believing I won't, my nose
so congested from crying I can barely
breathe.

I don't realize when day arrives until
Mama kneels beside me, home from
work, her gentle hand on my back,
that too-sweet perfume in the air,
and all my senses come back to
me again.

My head feels like a balloon about
to pop, too full of memories,
too heavy with disbelief.

How could Zee be gone?

The first day of all the days
to come without him, my eyes
unfocused, hands trembling,
hair standing on end, the drums
in the corner reminding me I'm
dreaming solo from now on.

PART II

The Blues

December 25

No Christmas Miracle

for us three, not for Mama,
Papa Zee, or me, no presents
peeled open beneath the tree,
no holiday music on the entire
floor, but flowers, teddy bears,
cards galore because people
know we're one heartbeat short.

I throw the digital metronome
that I handpicked against my
bedroom wall, watch it shatter
into pieces.

Mama knocks on my closed
door, but I can't move, can't
look her in the eye knowing
my promise wasn't the right
answer.

After a few minutes, she
shuffles back to her room,
the sigh of her mattress giving
way to her own hurt.

Funerals
are for the living.

I beg Mama not to make me
go after we attend the wake,
my heart raw from seeing Zee
that way.

The only thing sadder than
a child-size casket is seeing
it surrounded by people who
don't know what I hid about
the young boy dressed in his
tuxedo and red bow tie that
he wore a few days ago.

Like Ants Marching

into Papa Zee's apartment
after the funeral, well-meaning
people arrive with their dishes
in hand, their eyes cast down.

Papa Zee so dazed, Mama
and me step in to accept on his
behalf the food, the flowers,
the cards, the words like glass
breaking in my ears.

So sorry for your loss . . .
He's gone too soon . . .
Heaven gained an angel . . .
It's not the natural order of things . . .

I thank people I've never seen
before, from every floor it seems,
and a few I do recognize, like Ms.
González from down the hall,
who offers warm arroz con pollo and
leftover tamales from Christmas Eve.

The dining table fills with fried chicken,
tuna casserole, beef brisket, three kinds
of pie, and not a vegetable in sight.

I'm numb by the time Mr. Sanderson
arrives with an older gentleman on a
cane, another teacher from the school.
The one who called 911 when they found
Zee unresponsive.

Of all the people, Papa Zee speaks
to them, takes their hands in his and
mumbles appreciation for them trying
to save his son.

Sudden cardiac arrest in young people is so unexpected, the man
     with the cane says.
He was practicing alone in a classroom.
Wish we would have found him sooner.

I gave him CPR, Mr. Sanderson says, his voice cracking.
I'm so sorry it wasn't enough.

Sudden cardiac arrest.

That's what happened to that football
player Papa Zee told us about after
Zee fainted at school.

So much promise, he'd said. *Gone.*

Mr. Sanderson turns in my
direction, and my stomach
sinks. I hide in Zee's room
until he's gone, making me
feel even worse.

When the apartment is still
and quiet, half the day done,
Papa Zee, Mama, and I huddle
together, our three heads bobbing
in time with our tears.

Papa Zee

is up early one morning,
wandering the hallway, crying
so loudly that neighbors open
their doors to see about the
commotion and close them quick.

He's dressed for work, standing by
the elevator, when Mama approaches
with a gentle touch.

She steers him into our apartment,
takes off his coat and scarf, settles him
into her room, puts on a kettle for tea.

*Not yet, Zander. It's only been two weeks today.
Wait a little longer? For now, rest, sleep, eat.
That's all you have to do.*

I give Papa Zee a hug around the belly,
whisper, We *love you,* and although he
doesn't say anything back, I know he
feels the same.

Whiteout

to start the end of week two
without Zee, the school holiday
break a blur and distant memory.

It's a new year and nobody is
celebrating the blanket of pure
white snow outside.

I watch the winter wonderland
from my window as Papa Zee
trudges off to work, his first time
back on the worst weather day.

Mama's home and sleeping
and there's no school due
to the snow. I'm restless and
tired and missing the drums.

I cross the hall to face
a mountain of dirty dishes
collecting in the sink. I load
them in the dishwasher to
help Papa Zee before I
get to the drums.

There's a layer of dust settling
on the drums in the corner, but

I drape a sheet over them.
I so want to play,
but I can't bring myself
to shatter the quiet.

Time Changes

a lot of things, Mama says.

We huddle together in her room,
watch her small TV.

Like how when I was active duty, I couldn't be open about who
*   I loved.*
It took a good while, but Don't Ask, Don't Tell was eventually
*   repealed.*
Those times were painful to live through, that's for sure.

There's a sitcom on the screen that I don't
recognize, but Mama isn't paying attention
and neither am I. It's just keeping us company.

Mama pulls me to her,
hugs me tight.

My point is . . . this is painful too.
We're all missing Zee.
He was a good kid. Had a bright future.
Life throws curveballs
when we least expect them.
But time can help a lot of things.

I snuggle deeper into Mama,
pull the blanket up to my chin,
close my eyes.

Time is all I have.

First Family Night

with no music, no Zee, and
Mama trying hard to keep
it light, sharing stories about
work for a change.

Robin covered my shift when I took off from work . . .
Robin studied music at Berklee . . .
Robin asks about you all the time, Zander . . .

When she says *Robin,* her lips
turn up at the edges, eyes crinkle
in the corners from smiling so hard,
like she's remembering something
I can't recall.

It's not the only thing I notice tonight.

Papa Zee's food untouched, we help
clean the kitchen, put away the dishes
before Mama leads him by the elbow
to his bedroom, where he falls into bed
fully dressed.

I gather the two, three, four new washed casserole
dishes to store in Papa Zee's coat closet
and jump back when bunches of letters,
flyers, and pesky pamphlets tumble out
like pumpkin seeds from a jack-o'-lantern.

None of it is addressed to Zander Elliot Ellis Sr.

And now I know two things for sure:

Robin isn't going away

and

Papa Zee needs help.

Everybody Grieves

in their own way, Mama tells me
on Friday night when I ask why
she isn't as sad as Papa Zee.

Mama keeps carrying on,
going to work, checking in
on Papa Zee, spending time
with Robin like Zee wasn't
here one blink and gone the next.

I'm heartbroken, April. Truly, I am.
Some folks lose themselves when they lose someone they love.
It can be hard to want to carry on without that person in the
     world anymore.

After finding that mail in his closet,
it's been hard for me to focus this week
at school, at home harder to stay awake.
Once the sun sets, I just want
the day to be over.

Papa Zee is the closest thing
to Zee I have left, and I'll do
whatever I can to help him
until he's feeling better.

I promised Zee I wouldn't tell
and now look at Papa Zee.

No matter how long it takes,
I've got an idea that might help,
and at least I have to try.

My Test Run

starts the very next day.

A Saturday morning with a
single piece of mail I pluck
from the pile in Papa Zee's
closet.

Once Mama is home from
work, asleep and snoring,
I sneak off to Fisher Street
for my first attempt
to help Papa Zee.

I remember this street best
because of that older lady
who baked cookies, handed
Papa Zee and me small sacks
of oatmeal raisin still warm from
the oven that day when he took
me to work with him.

That and when she smiled,
she had only three teeth.

Papa Zee and me munched all
day on the cookies and he laughed
when I wiped the crumbs from his
beard.

This is a benefit of the job
that nobody mentions, he'd said.

I drop off my single letter on
Fisher Street, feeling pretty
good about my plan so far.

I got you, Papa Zee.

Asa's Waiting

outside of the school for me
first thing Tuesday morning.

When I returned to school after
winter recess, she had still been
away.

Her face lights up when she
sees me. By the way she squints,
I can see the questions forming in
her head.

I wish I had the energy to be
as excited.

Wanna walk together? she asks.

I shrug my shoulders,
start walking to class,
not feeling very much
like talking.

I drift to our room, to my seat,
hoping she can see now is not
a good time.

But Asa's curiosity gets the best of her.

I'm sorry about Zander, she says finally.
Were you with him when he died?
Did you get his violin? Do you ever try to play it?

I spend the morning swatting her questions
away like pesky flies.

Asa tries to beat out a rhythm
on her desk to draw me in,
but her attempt only sets me
more on edge.

Her attention smothering.

When the teacher turns
from writing on the board,
my hand shoots up to
excuse myself to
the bathroom.

I race from the room,
lock myself in a stall,
make myself as small
as possible.

The hole inside me from missing
Zee feels like it's growing.

It's been almost a month
since we last walked to school
together, since we had our first
snowball fight to start the winter.

I scream, *Why, why, why,* using
toilet paper to wipe my
tears and blow my nose.

Screaming feels good, but it won't
bring Zee back. Someone in heels
bursts through the bathroom door,
checking every stall for feet.

As the last notes of my words echo
off the barren walls and fall silent,
the stranger pushes open my door
to find me.

Mrs. Dial,
our fifth-grade teacher
and my favorite so far,
treated Zee and me like
we mattered, her words
always kind, her hands
always warm.

Come with me, she says, *we should talk.*

Mrs. Dial, not much taller
than I am, with a full head
of gray hair, leads me past
my classroom.

She nods at Ms. Chisholm,
and when Asa notices us,
I look right through her.

I keep step with Mrs. Dial, who chooses
a corner of the gymnasium a few steps
up in the bleachers for just us two.

I miss him so much, Mrs. Dial. Like, every minute of every day.
I keep thinking it's a bad dream and I'm going to wake up.
But every day is the same as the day before.
He's still gone and I'm never going to see him again.

Mrs. Dial holds my hand as she listens.

Loss is never easy, April.
I know this is hard. Your life has changed.
It might lead to other changes too.
Here's what I want you to know . . .

She takes a long, deep breath,
scoots closer to me, drapes her arm
over my shoulders.

All change leads to something different.
Different isn't always easy, nor is it always bad.
It's just different. And getting used to anything different takes time.
Do you understand?

I nod, wondering if she and
Mama met over coffee or something,
their words so similar.

Know what else? I ask, leaning closer.
I don't know what to do about Asa Curtis.

Mrs. Dial removes her arm,
leans back, her lips a straight,
tight line.

What do you mean? I don't follow.

She's sort of cool. All that scout stuff she does.
But also sort of clueless. And she misses a lot of school.
It's hard to have a friend at school who keeps disappearing
    all the time.

I stop myself and sit upright.
Did I just call Asa Curtis a friend?

Have you ever asked her?
About missing so much school?

I shake my head no, sheepishly.

Maybe you should. That's what a friend would do.
Everyone has their own burdens, April.
If you ever want to talk more about what you're
feeling, you know where to find me.

Mrs. Dial stands up, adjusts her skirt,
starts down the bleacher stairs.

She reaches out a hand to steady me
as I join her on the gym floor.

Better? Mrs. Dial asks.

Better. Thank you.

I do feel a little lighter, though
the heaviness comes back before
I've even reached my classroom.

Blue

is the color
of the sky today,
the car driving by,
the streak in a
neighbor's hair.

Blue is also the color
of the roses on the
kitchen table when I
arrive home from school,
too cheery to be something
Mama picked, too creepy
to be found in nature,
the note attached in
large loopy letters:

Thinking of you, Chantelle.
With open arms,

Robin

After almost two months, silly me
thought she'd lost interest
or Mama came to her senses and
realized there's no room in our lives
for her.

Blue is the color of all my feelings.

Quick as Lightning,

Mama removes the flowers
and card from the table before
I've even made it to my room,
shed my school clothes, and
taken the first deep breath
of the day.

How was school?

I stretch out on my bed,
stare at my Drum Mavens,
wishing they would tell me
what to do now.

Hard.

Do I ask about Robin?
Do I wait for her to tell me?
Do I go across the hall to keep
Papa Zee company?

Mama is at my door in three
long steps, her expression as
unfamiliar as those creepy blue
roses.

Hard because of your subjects or . . .
Come talk to me. Dinner's ready.

It's family night, but Papa Zee
asked to pass on dinner and we
eat so much earlier now anyway.

I fall asleep once the sun sets,
only to wake up when the moon
is still high in the sky.

Everywhere I turn feels awkward,
off-balance, with Asa, with Papa Zee,
with Mama too.

Do you honestly want to know?

Mama pushes around the pork
chop and peas on her plate.

I can't remember the last time
she baked anything, making the
apartment smell like home.

I wouldn't have asked if I didn't.

I tell her the one truth that
feels safe to share.

*There's a classmate who
was being super nosy and*

wouldn't stop talking.
Mrs. Dial helped me out.

I don't mention that I was
hiding out in the bathroom,
screaming out my feelings.

Questions about Zee?

I nod my head, my turn to push
the food around my plate.

Mama waits for me to say more,
but I'm at a loss for words.

After more than ten minutes in silence,
Mama finishes her food, rises to rinse
her plate before loading it in the dishwasher.

Thank you for sharing, April.
This is hard for us all.

I *know.*

Mama rubs my back and smiles,
then disappears into her room.

An hour later, as I'm drifting into sleep, the sound of her soft laughter behind her door makes me wonder whether I'll ever laugh again.

I grab my things and leave.

Across the Hall

I find Papa Zee staring into
Zee's room, and I know that
look, that feeling, that need
to see Zee again wiping down
his violin, flipping that stupid
foam basketball at the closet
hoop.

I got one for you, Papa Zee.
What do you get when you drop a piano on an army base?
A flat major. Get it? Good one, right?

Papa Zee doesn't blink an eye.

How about I play you something?

He moves from the door to the sofa,
and I pull the drums from their corner,
grab a nearby sweatshirt to wipe
away the dust, check my seat, and
realize I don't have my sticks.

I left them across the hall.

Makes no difference anyway.
Papa Zee is still staring into space,
and moving the drums into position

to play makes my stomach hurt,
reminds me of the last time
Zee and me played together.

I sink down to the floor next
to Papa Zee, waiting on him
to retreat to his bedroom.

That doesn't take long at all.

Once his door is closed, light off,
I check his closet again for mail.

Papa Zee Leaves

in the morning like normal,
dressed to deliver his mail,
but it's clear by the mounting
stash in his closet that he's
not working through his grief,
not working at all.

Now the pile is as tall as a fire
hydrant, spouting more mail
every day.

I keep thinking about the people
who are waiting for a bill, a letter,
something they ordered long ago.

When he's in his room for the night,
and after I've finished my homework,
I look up the street names, not a
dozen blocks from here.

Easy enough to get to by foot,
if I leave school a little early.
It's the one thing I can do in
Zee's memory, the only thing
I can offer Papa Zee as he keeps
vanishing before my eyes.

Things Overheard

in the school bathroom are
enough to make me scream,
again, but that won't help
me feel any better.

While I'm changing clothes
in a stall, preparing to deliver
Papa Zee's mail, I hear . . .

Did you know that boy who used to go here?
You think that girl he was friends with will stay?
What if one of us goes to school and never goes home again?

I charge out of the stall, shocking them
into silence. The two older girls scurry out
of the bathroom so fast one drops her
lip gloss but doesn't dare turn around
to pick it up.

They didn't know Zee
and they don't know me.
I wipe a tear about to fall
but don't delay too long
because I have work to do.

Delivering Mail

is harder than it looks.

My back sore from
stuffing as much
mail as possible
into my backpack.

I cut my last two classes
thinking it would be
plenty of time, but now
it feels like I bit off more
than I can chew.

Names don't always match boxes,
some boxes need a key,
plenty of boxes too small to
fit all the undelivered mail,
some too tall to reach, and
so many addresses inside
office buildings on one single
street that I don't dare enter.

Who wouldn't notice a young
Black girl delivering mail in late
afternoon on a school day?

I'm trying to help Papa Zee,
not get him in trouble.

I'm short, not invisible, and
before I know it, I run out
of time.

All the Mail

I can't deliver I push into
blue mailboxes I pass as
I start home, hoping when
it gets back to the post office
they'll give it to somebody
other than Papa Zee to deliver.

The thought of Mama noticing
the time starts me jogging
before breaking into a sprint,
hoping to get back home
soon.

The temperature keeps dropping,
but I reach home drenched in sweat,
prepared to pull off my coat, kick off
my shoes, and take a long hot bath.

I see those ugly blue flowers are back
on the kitchen table, front and center,
when I wished Mama would keep them
in her room.

And something new.

Robin Is

in my apartment,
at my table, waiting
on me to say something,
like I'm the one who's
out of place.

It was one thing for her to show up
at Papa Zee's, but seeing her in
our space makes me feel
awkward. Again.

I hear Mama rustling in her room,
so I know she's home.

Hello, April. I know it's been a while.
It's nice to see you again.

Alone with that woman
who has stolen Mama's heart,
I forget my manners, storm
by her without a word, into my
bedroom to make sure nothing
has been disturbed, not a single thing
out of order.

I pretend to read a book from
my shelf, ignoring their muffled
voices, spontaneous laughter,

and long sighs, figuring if I stall
long enough she will leave.

After almost an hour, there's a
knock on our door, the smell of
pizza wafting in the air.

I worked up an appetite delivering
mail, and my stomach grumbles.

Time to face the music.

Lucky Number Three

doesn't feel so lucky seeing
Robin for the third time in
Papa Zee's apartment, each
time hoping it would be
the last.

We bring the pizza with us,
two large bottles of soda,
and there is nothing shocking
or celebratory like her last two
visits.

The only weird thing is having family
dinner on a Wednesday for a change.

I'm so sorry about your son, Robin starts.
I know the card and flowers I sent are little consolation.
I thought I'd bring something else.

It's been three months since
she was last here and almost
four weeks since Zee died.

Robin presses a button on her phone,
and a familiar song fills the room with music for the first
time in what feels like forever.

It's one of Papa Zee's favorites,
"Lean on Me" by Bill Withers.

"Sometimes in our lives
We all have pain
We all have sorrow . . ."
The acoustic guitar and lyrics stir
something in me, remind me how
much I miss hearing music
and playing it.

From the looks of it, the music
moves Papa Zee too. He eats
two whole slices of pizza, taps his
fingers on the table, shakes his leg
like he wants to stand up but doesn't.

Even Mama notices, her expression
soft, her eyes damp. She reaches across
the table to rub his hand.

He looks a little less sad, a little more
like the man I remember from before.

When Robin leaves and Mama goes to work,
I'm going to fill up my backpack with all the
mail that'll fit and try again tomorrow to keep
helping Papa Zee.

Nighttime

is the worst time, when Mama
is off to work, Papa Zee is
asleep, and all I want to do
is play the drums.

Hearing music tonight has me
itching to play.

The Next Day

I slip into the library to watch
videos again before I prepare
for my early departure.

That's when I notice Asa, who
hasn't been in class for a week,
walking with two white adults,
a man in a blue suit two sizes too big,
a woman in a summer dress even though
it's thirty degrees outside.

All stepping into the school office,
heads down, faces solemn.

I want to call out to her, but I've got
more mail today than ever before,
and less time to deliver it.

I wonder if she lost someone too?

Life Without Zee

feels like time moving fast
and slow, my memories of
him suspended like a butterfly
in glass.

That's what I'm thinking while I'm
delivering the mail, trying to keep
warm, though my hands and toes
feel like ice cubes.

There's a woman outside a
church handing out steaming
cups of something hot.

When she motions me over,
I don't hesitate.

She stares at me funny, and I
realize too late it's the woman
from Fisher Street who gave
Papa Zee and me those
fresh-baked cookies.

I *remember you. Zander's little girl, right?*
Haven't seen him around lately. How is he?

She smiles, bright white dentures
blinding me, and I choke on the cider,

fearing my time is short to help
Papa Zee before someone else
recognizes me, before he can get
back on his feet.

He's taking a little time for himself.
It's super cold today. So cold.

And ain't even February yet. But Boston weather?
Give it a minute. It'll change.

I sip down the warm liquid as slow
as possible, trying to make it last.

Thanks for this. I better get home.

I'm off again, making another mail dump
nearest home, arriving to the apartment
fifteen minutes later than the last time.

It's dark as midnight outside.

When I exit the elevator, the perfume
hits me before I hear the laughter.

Papa Zee's door closed,
mine wide open, spilling
light to greet me home.

The Drums

are what I notice before
Robin notices me.

Mama's back to the door,
her head falling forward
with the last notes of
laughter in her voice.

The drums sit in our living
room where the side table
should be, the red velvet
love seat pushed far to the
right to make room.

The drums!

Mama turns to face me,
her expression soft, her
voice softer.

Zander can't take having those in his place any longer.
It's too hard on him. And they won't play themselves.

We stare at the drums
that are now under our roof,
our quiet, orderly home,
completely out of order.

But you don't like noise, remember?
Silence is golden and all that?

Mama pauses, and Robin slides
her hand across
the table to Mama's, both their heads
bowed low.

That's still true. But if you really want to play, April . . .

I haven't moved from the doorway,
but my palms itch, my fingers tingle,
because this is the very thing I've wanted.
But Zee isn't here to see it.

There's an anxious feeling in my
stomach that I can't ignore.

Music was something I shared
with Papa Zee and Zee, me
without them doesn't feel right.

I pluck one stick from the
windowsill in my room and
make a sad attempt to start
a beat.

Mama shifts forward in
her seat, Robin does too,
like they're expecting a show.

It's too much to wrap
my mind around, so I drop
my stick to the floor, walk
to my bedroom, and shut
the door, tight.

Three Good Things

this second week of February
that turn the tide of hope:

I play the drums just a little
when Mama isn't home. I don't
feel as bad about cutting school
early after so many weeks.

Mama dating Robin means she's
preoccupied when I return every
evening a little later than the day
before.

By Friday, Papa Zee says he's
in the mood for sharing, so I bring
over our favorite chocolate milk
while he finds some Golden Oreos
deep in the cupboard.

I settle into the sofa beside
him, ignoring the egg-crate
foam peeling from the walls,
and wait on him to start.

Did I Ever Tell You

how I met Zander's mother?

He's never told me this before,
and if he's going to tell this story,
I'm hoping he'll also talk about the mail,
how the pile keeps dwindling in
his closet.

His eyes wet and distant,
I know better than to mention
it now.

I saw her playing outside the Ruggles T station.
I was working as a bouncer at Slades.
I told her she should try to get a gig.

She was truly something else. So smart and talented.
It was Samantha who said I needed a regular job.
That was after she got pregnant. So, I took the post-office exam.

Now look at me.

No Samantha.
No Zander Jr.
No nothing.

I stop dunking my cookies
in the milk.

You got us. We're still here.
And work. How's work going?

He stares through me, like
he hasn't heard the question.

I've been here since I was a young man.
Following a dream that went nowhere.
Might be time for something new.

Papa Zee doesn't wait for me
to reply, his grief like a shade
drawing down for the night.

He lumbers to his room, closes
his door, same as every night
since Zee's been gone, us both
alone and lonely.

25 Calumet Street

is an unfamiliar address
on an unfamiliar street,
far enough away from the
prying eyes of people who
might recognize me, might
spoil the gift I'm giving Papa Zee
without him even knowing.

This address has two big
bundles of mail, more than
half my backpack to one
single address, held tight by
rubber bands.

Every piece that's not junk
is threatening—

DO NOT IGNORE

OVERDUE

FINAL NOTICE

The house has a bright orange
door, the front garden's
withering gray stalks
look like they could have
been sunflowers.

The stair planks are loose, the screen
door crooked on the hinge, the dingy
curtains have Sesame Street characters.
There's someone screaming so loud
it's a wonder I didn't hear it down the street.

I slide the two bundles beneath
the box because it's hanging on
by one nail. I am almost to the
sidewalk when I'm caught.

Stop right there! Come back here, girl.

I bite my lower lip, feel the blood
rushing to my ears. The woman in
the doorway is pale and thin, her eyes
glassy, a robe hanging off her slight frame.

Ain't you a little young to be delivering mail?

There's a crashing sound behind her,
then a high-pitched scream. I'm so
nervous I start walking backward,
close enough to the sidewalk again
that I could run.

A man stumbles through the door
in boxer shorts, knocking into her,

his feet and chest bare, long scars
along his legs, eyes bloodshot and
bugged out.

I've seen enough. Before I can bolt,
a girl pushes past them both, trying
to stuff them back inside.

But it's too late.

I've seen the three. They've seen me.

She swipes the two bundles
from beside the door, and for
once, Asa Curtis is speechless.

My Mind Keeps Playing

tricks on me, telling me
that was another white
girl who looks like Asa
Curtis but maybe wasn't
her at all.

I twist and turn all night long
remembering the redness in
Asa's cheeks when she saw
who was standing outside her
house.

Trying my best to remember
if those were the same people
I saw at the school with her.

I promise myself before I drift off
to sleep that when Asa shows up
at school again, I'll be a better
classmate, a less fickle friend.

No Mail Today

because after second
period, I get called to the
principal's office instead.
Mama's already there, arms
folded. Eyes still sleepy.

She's up five hours earlier
than usual.

Mr. Arnold hands Mama
tea when she only drinks
coffee black, but she accepts
the steaming cup without a
single look in my direction.

It appears Ms. Jackson has been departing school early.

Mr. Arnold reviews a book flat open
on his desk, his booming voice too
loud for this cramped office.

According to our records, she's cut school seven times since the
*   New Year.*
What do you have to say for yourself, young lady?

Mama turns her full attention
on me and my shoulders hunch
to my ears.

I want to say maybe Zee would still
be here if I'd spoken up, Papa Zee
wouldn't be vanishing before my
eyes, but I don't expect clueless Mr.
Arnold understands what it feels like
to lose a best friend.

I'm still sad about Zee.

Mr. Arnold leans back in his chair,
clears his throat three times.

That's understandable, Ms. Jackson. To still be grieving.
It doesn't explain why you leave school before the day is done.
If you aren't here and you aren't at home, where do you go?

I fold my arms now, plant my feet solid
on the floor, even though I can feel
Mama's frustration and disappointment
filling the room like smoke.

Outside. To get air.
It's hard to focus sometimes.

I see. The next time you need air you are welcome to go to the
   nurse's office.
But cutting school is unacceptable. Do you understand?

Mama returns the tea
untouched to Mr. Arnold's
desk, stands to leave.

She understands. Don't you, April?

I don't know what's worse:

Mama called into school,
disrupting her sleep schedule.

or

Me going back to class knowing
what's awaiting me at home.

I'm So Nervous

about facing Mama after school,
I move slower than a sloth to get home
even though the wind chill is below zero.

As I approach my building,
another resident pushes
past me in a huff, and I let
them go ahead, missing
two elevators on purpose.

I linger in the musty, wet
lobby, stretching what
little time I have left before
facing Mama again.

What's Waiting

for me when I step out
of the elevator is not what
I'm expecting at all.

It's Valentine's Day and Papa Zee
asked to skip family dinner again,
but there's something savory and sweet
in the air. I rush to the apartment.

There's a roasted chicken on the table,
rice pilaf, green beans, a sweet potato pie.

Mama is nowhere in sight.

It's my favorite meal, and Mama
knows it because she only makes
it when I'm nervous before a big test.

Her bedroom door creaks open,
and she leads the way with
Robin following, both looking
so serious that I sit at the table,
quick.

Mama and Robin take their seats,
fill up their plates. I do the same,
keeping my mouth shut until my plate
is bone clean.

I *want to be clear, it's not okay to cut school, April.*
But I've *been distracted lately. And so much has happened.*
We *made this meal to say I'll do better, and we'll do better together.*
I *hope that's okay.*

You *both made it? I ask. All of it?*

I *don't bake,* Robin says, touching Mama's elbow.
But I *can hold my own in the kitchen.*

Mama might have changed
in some ways, but not in any of the
ways that matter most.

I Relax

too soon, all the good vibes
still hanging in the air, when
Mama and Robin share
a mysterious smirk.

Robin eases from the table
and settles herself behind the
drums, pulls a pair of sticks from
behind her back, and starts a
simple beat so easy I can tell
she's done this before.

Am I doing it right?

I rush to move her out the way,
off the stool, snatch the sticks from
her manicured fingernails.

No! This is how you play the drums!

I close my eyes and find the rhythm,
my body relaxes, the vibrations I love
in the palms of my hands, the soles of
my feet, and everything starts to fall
away.

It always feels so amazing to play,
to find my flow, the discomfort

in my stomach fading with
each strike of my stick.

I'm playing the drums,
in my own apartment,
with Mama as my witness.

Never thought I'd see this day.

A Small Moment

of hope surfaces as I stare
at my Drum Mavens, the full moon
casting a spotlight on my rug.

I ignore the sound of dishes
being cleared, food stored in
the fridge, and stand in the beam.

I bow before my imaginary audience.

It doesn't take long for my old feelings
of doubt to return, reminding me
whatever progress I've made toward
my dream is stuck without Zee's support
and Papa Zee's lessons.

No Escaping

school early today or
any other day now to
deliver mail.

Asa refuses to look at me,
but I try to talk to her when
the teacher turns to write on the board.

So, you live on Calumet Street?

Asa twists her body away from
me, faces the door instead.

It doesn't feel one bit good to
be on the receiving end of a
cold shoulder.

I'm Sure Now

it was Asa, seeing her head
down, mouth clamped shut
all morning long.

I wonder how many times
Mr. and Mrs. Curtis have
been called to Mr. Arnold's
office, how many cups of tea
he's made for them to drink.

I remember what Mrs. Dial said.
People and their burdens.
How we all have them.

Second Try

at lunch with Asa,
who has no lunch,
not from home or
school, who sits
biting at her nails,
alone.

I don't know the right words
to say, and I have too many
questions to even know
where to start.

I join her with my slice of pizza,
carton of milk, red apple.

Has it always been like that at your house?

She takes the apple from my tray,
wipes it on her wrinkled shirt
until it has a perfect shine,
then takes a big bite like she
hasn't eaten in days.

And I let her.

Class Project #4:
a science experiment.
I ask Ms. Chisholm if I can
be Asa's partner, and when she
agrees, I ease to the back of the
room to get our supplies:

an empty glass bottle, glitter,
a funnel, three cups of water.

Reading the directions on
the board, I use the funnel
to slide the glitter in the bottle,
and Asa finally starts whispering,
loud enough for me to hear.

No, it hasn't always been this way. My daddy drives trucks.
Last September his semi jackknifed when a car cut him off.

I add the water, put the lid on
the bottle, and seal it tight.

He broke his back, both knees, a bunch of other bones.
Everything, he kept saying, hurt.

I turn the bottle upside down,
quickly move it in a circular motion

before setting it down to watch the
sparkly tornadoes erupt on our table
and others across the room.

That's when he started taking the blue pills.
For the pain, he said, that didn't get better after his body healed.
I flush them down the toilet. But he always seems to get more.

Asa doesn't even notice what's
happening around the room,
she's swirling so hard in her
own story vortex.

When I'm not here, I'm watching my brother and sister.
It helps when my mom is out interviewing for work.

I'm only half listening to the
teacher as she tries to explain
centripetal force.

He's still not driving. And he gets angry a lot.
He didn't used to before.

Asa calmly slides down in
her seat, leaving me sad
and dumbstruck.

When I Find

my words again, my curiosity
now gets the best of me.

Is there anything I can do?

Asa folds into herself,
pretends she didn't hear,
and stares out the window
for the rest of class.

When the bell rings, the class erupts
in noise, screeching chairs, scrambling
feet, voices talking over one another.

I follow her out into the hallway.

You still play the drums?

I nod, waiting for her
to launch into a blizzard of
other questions, but I can see
from her eyes she's got nothing
more to say.

Wally's Cafe

is a subway ride away from
home. Yesterday was a holiday
and this week is February recess, so
we're going out for family night
for a change.

I tell Papa Zee where we're going,
sure he'll want to come along, but
he's dressed in ratty pajama pants
and a worn sweatshirt, and has no
intention of leaving the house.

It's Mama, Robin, and me.

I'm distracted and still feeling heavy
thinking about what Asa said
at school, remembering the scene
the last time I delivered mail.
Robin yammers on about
Wally's, this Boston institution
where she's taking us tonight.

We travel the Orange Line and
exit at the Massachusetts Ave. stop.

The wind whips around us as we
walk. We pull our coats tighter,

hats lower, only steps from the
storefront with the bright red door,
bars on the window, dozens of
people milling about outside,
smoking, and using their breath
to keep hands warm.

With one nod from Robin,
a man opens the door, and
the sound of music knocks
me over, clearing my thoughts
as we push through the wall of
people to get inside.

It's dark and cramped
in a space no bigger than
our living room, so hot
and stuffy that it's hard
to breathe.

I glimpse a band on a platform
stage between the gaps of
arms and legs.

There's a woman on drums,
her locs thick and swinging,
hiding her face, but there's no

mistaking those hands are
making beats unlike any I've
ever heard before.

I'm swimming in the rhythm,
riding the waves of the drums
as they carry the trumpet, the
guitar, the keyboard.

This is way better than any
YouTube video.

This is music with a soul, a heartbeat
lifting me up, making me remember
why I wanted to make music
of my own.

Feet tapping, bodies swaying,
fingers snapping, clapping between
solos, sweat pouring from the
drummer's face, neck, and arms.

One day, that's going to be me.

I'm Not Sleepy

at all when we get home,
too wound up from Wally's.

I use the key beneath the mat
to let myself into Papa Zee's
apartment, and it's worse than
usual, not a single surface clear
or clean.

I gather his clothes to
make a single pile, bus
the dishes to the kitchen
sink, wrangle the potato chip,
cookie, and ice cream wrappers
into the overflowing trash.

Before I even turn the knob
to the coat closet, I know what
I'll find: a fresh stash of mail
on the floor, three coats that
once were Zee's, swinging and
lonely.

Papa Zee is in his room,
sound asleep and snoring.

There's no other way I can help
Papa Zee. I should have told

him about Zee's racing heart.
Maybe Zee would still be here
if I had, but I've done all I can.
I'm not ready yet, but soon
I'm coming clean.

I sneak into Zee's room,
push aside the cardboard
boxes that must be packed
with Zee's things because
the room is otherwise bare.

I fall into his bed, the scent
of his coconut hair grease still
faint on his pillow.

My Dreams

are nonstop moments
of Zee standing at our
intersection, playing the
violin with his eyes closed,
a tiny casket beside his feet,
open for spare change.

I awake with a start
to Mama knocking on
Zee's bedroom door,
telling me it's time to
cross the hall.

The dream still lingers,
leaving me wondering if
Zee would have made it
big with his talent, his hard
work.

If that would have been his future,
and thanks to keeping his secret,
now I'll never know.

After February Recess

I keep a beat running through
my head, tapping through my fingers
all through class, through
lunch, and trips to the
bathroom and back.

Asa notices and she taps
out beats with me between
class periods, mimicking what
I do, and then it's my turn.

Feels nice to have a friend again,
though no one can compare to Zee.

I'm eager to get back home
after school to talk to Papa Zee,
to start my journey back to playing
the drums for real.

I'm Confused

when I return home from school,
check for the spare key
beneath the welcome mat,
open Papa Zee's door wide
to find an empty apartment.

No note.

No mail in the closet.

Every room clean and barren.

All that's left are stray
pieces of egg-crate foam
crumpled in the corner of
the living room.

I rush across the hall.

For as long as I can remember
I've moved from one apartment
to the other, both places welcoming
me with open arms. Not even three
months since Zee's passing and
another thing has changed.

Mama Appears

from the bathroom, eyes so
puffy she won't look at me,
so we both focus on Zee's violin,
lifeless on our kitchen table.

Where . . . is . . . Papa . . . Zee?

She lights the kettle on the stove.
I watch the flames lick the cold
metal, afraid if I ask again my tears
will start and wash us both away.

Zander moved out this afternoon.
He said he couldn't heal staying here.
Too many memories.
He's gone back to New Orleans.

She pushes Zee's violin
in its soft gray case across
the table to me.

He left this for you.
He thought you should have it.

How could I have failed to
save both Zee and Papa Zee?

I look away from Mama, but I can
tell she's trying to catch my eye.

The weight of our memories
harder than ever to carry.

The New Normal

means Robin stays
overnight with me while
Mama goes to work.

I keep my distance, feeling
dazed and guilty that I never
told Papa Zee the truth.

I spend every night in my room
studying the faces of my Drum Mavens.
No family dinners, no playing
drums, but falling asleep to the sounds
of jazz in my earbuds on repeat,
waiting for morning to come.

Thunder Snow

jolts me awake one night,
three weeks after the new
normal begins.

Spring recess is almost here.

There's a low, soft whine of violin
strings playing somewhere nearby.

I pinch myself, thinking I must be
dreaming, but the goose bumps
along my arms tell me different.

I inch from my bed, crack open
the door to find Robin playing
Zee's violin.

She's playing a song I don't know
so slowly and beautifully, my eyes
water.

I stand in the doorway appreciating
her playing before remembering that
is Zee's violin.

Put it down! That's not yours! Put it down!

The tears come faster than I can
wipe them away, and my vision blurs,
nose runs, heart aches like someone
reached into my chest and squeezed.

She slips the violin from beneath
her chin, rests it on the table, kneels,
and opens her arms wide.

I cry harder, start to hiccup
until I tip forward into her waiting
embrace, and she holds me,
rocks me, welcomes me to . . .

Let it out. It's okay. Let it all out now.

It takes so long for my hiccups
to stop, my eyes to dry, my nose
to breathe clear again that my feet
have fallen asleep, tingle something
crazy.

I step back to look with fresh eyes at this
woman with the kind face, gap-tooth smile,
and platinum-blond curls who has taken up
space uninvited in my life.

Robin

makes us both cups
of steaming hot cocoa.

I used to be a lot like you.
Loved playing music but wasn't always consistent.

The unusual weather creates
a show outside, flashes of
light, the sky a curtain of white.

It wasn't until I found the right teacher that I hit my stride.
She taught multiple instruments, not only strings.
My brother took drum lessons with her.
He shared what he learned sometimes.
That's how I know a little about the drums.

I'm still skeptical about her,
a woman who would play a
dead boy's instrument without
permission.

And you don't play anymore?
You ever played at Wally's?

I tuck Zee's violin back in the case,
slip the bow in its place, zipper
it closed.

Regina and I played there when we were at Berklee.
She was the woman on the drums.
I love playing music. Always will.

Life is a lot busier these days with work and family.

I nod, make a mental note
about Regina, and thank
Robin for the cocoa.

We going to be okay, you and me? she asks.

I walk Zee's violin back to my
room for safekeeping, holding
back a smile as I close the door.

If you take me back to Wally's soon?
Maybe.
Good night.

No School Today

and Mama's worn out
from the total whiteout
she said turned her
twenty-minute commute
home into two hours.

As the plows whoosh through
falling snow on the street below,
I'm curious about how Asa is
doing, remembering that crooked
screen door, those bedsheets
in the window, neither
any match for this cold.

No drum playing while Mama's
asleep and I've got nothing better
to do than my homework.

First Day Back

to school after two snow
days, feeling more restless
than ever about the drums . . .
Robin . . .
Asa . . .
life.

Asa arrives early to school
with dark circles beneath her
eyes, nails bit to the quick.

You want to talk later? I ask,
keeping my voice low.

Asa ignores the teacher,
turns her whole body to
talk to me like we aren't in
the middle of class.

Don't you miss Zander?
Not just miss him, but, like . . .
miss what it was like . . .
being with him.

Ms. Chisholm's ears perk up.

She leaves her desk to position
herself between ours.

We can talk after class if you like? she offers.

We both shake our heads no
and turn to face the board.

I try again, whispering.

Of course I do. All the time.

Asa's eyes water, mine
start too. Tears stream
down our faces.

He was always nice to me.

I wipe my eyes first.

Asa wipes hers on one
sleeve, her nose on the other.

Zee was the sun,
I was the moon, and
neither of us paid much

attention to the rest of
the solar system.

Not even the stars.

Or so I thought.

Zee was that kind of special.

What I Know

about Asa Curtis could
fit in a thimble.

When the last bell rings,
Asa gathers her stuff
and doesn't look back.

I fast-walk to catch up, keep
in step with her as we near
the main exit.

Want to come to my house this weekend? I ask.

I can't. Have to babysit my brother and sister.

Okay, maybe next week after school? I try again.

. . . . . .

She keeps moving through
the crowd until she's on the
bus, eyes straight ahead.

Did I say something wrong?

After School

I'm convinced it's now
or never, so I go to
Zee's old school, wander
the halls, and hope I'll find
Mr. Sanderson.

There's no music spilling
from classrooms today.

I pause outside the auditorium,
then throw the doors open,
race down the aisle, gathering my
courage as I reach the
massive, empty stage.

This is where Zee played his solo.

I notice a black X taped on the stage,
climb up to stand on the X, look out
into the sea of seats knowing this is
what Zee saw that day.

I imagine what it feels like to
get a standing ovation, allow
myself to feel my sticks
in my hands, air drum my favorite
combination, my daydream peeking
into view.

I'm brought back to the present
by a figure at the back of the
room: Mr. Sanderson, clearing
his throat before he slips back
into the hallway.

I'm already off the stage, racing
toward the exit to find him, and
there he is at the double doors to
the school, this time with something
in his hand.

This is how you can reach me.
I'm assuming you're ready for lessons?

He offers me a piece of paper
and I stuff it in my bookbag.

We must leave now, he says.
They're closing the building.
April . . . I'm happy you came.

As soon as I'm home, safe
in my room, I fold the paper,
slip it into my favorite
Drum! magazine,
pretending it's more
precious than gold.

School Days

are hard without Zee,
but harder now without Zee
and Asa.

She's been absent four days,
and the hours drag on even though
I know what's going on with her.

The only good thing about
this school week is it's short.
No school tomorrow, to celebrate
Good Friday, and I know exactly
what can help me feel better.

Another Night

alone in my room, but each
day brings sunlight a bit
longer than the day before,
and my eyes are less heavy
with sleep.

I wait thirty minutes
after Mama leaves for work
before I knock on her bedroom door
to remind Robin about Wally's.

I want to get closer this time,
want to study Regina's style.

What would your mother say?

I give Robin my best puppy-dog eyes,
clasp my hands together,
prepared to stay this way
until she gives in.

It takes thirty seconds.

Okay. Let's go. Most musicians are night owls anyway.
Welcome to the club.

The clock on the oven reads
nine thirty, a full hour before
my bedtime, but I grab my sticks
hoping Regina might sign them.

Second Trip

to Wally's and I don't
waste the chance to ask
Robin about music school.

You want me to lie or tell you the truth?

A group of college students board the train
making a ruckus, and I tune them out
to hear Robin better.

The truth, please.

It was demanding. And competitive.
Every student put in years of lessons and practice.
Nobody stumbles upon greatness. You must work for it.

I hear echoes of what Zee
always said about hard work,
how he didn't just talk about it,
he did it.

If our dream was a race, he was well
on his way, while my feet feel glued to
the starting line.

Same Place, Different

band at Wally's, still hazy
and dark, crowded, no
Regina in sight.

This time I squeeze through
the bodies, and Robin follows
me as we post ourselves along
the wall nearest the stage, Robin
reaching down to find my hand.

She slips me two neon-orange
earplugs, quick and easy. I stick
them in my ears and feel the music,
more muted now but still pounding
through my body.

Tonight the band has an
upright bass and guitar,
keyboard and drums, the
melody more rock than jazz.

Every song has four solos,
so each musician shows off,
and the songs feel forever long,
but I lean in closer every time
the drummer gets a solo.

Robin taps her foot on the
two-and-four beat, I choose
the one-and-three,
two musicians in flow.

All Weekend Long

we head off to Wally's
after Mama goes to work,
never the same band twice,
and still no sign of Regina.

I learn a little more each
visit, an order to playing the
drums I never noticed before.

Each drummer carries the
power to bring everything
else together onstage.

Holding the sticks easy
and light, body loose
and attuned to every other
instrument.

I clutch my sticks with closed
fists when I play, tight like
they might flutter away.

First adjust the seat,
sit straight—no slouching
allowed—before each begins.

I get every drummer to sign
my sticks, and even the club
regulars smile and nod to
encourage me, the only kid
in a room full of giants.

Robin and I drag ourselves
away each night after midnight,
scurry for the last T home,
both hard asleep when Mama
arrives the next morning.

I've Lost Track
of time, nights and days
start to blur together when
it used to feel like seconds
crept along like ice melting
on a cold day.

I don't recognize this
new life, still evolving,
but it's not all bad.

Mama, Robin, and me
eat together now most
nights. Robin teaching
me what she knows on
the drums, her playing,
then me trying to repeat.

Mama's fully on board now,
hanging pink egg-crate foam
to pad the walls to help dampen
the sound.

No need to get thrown out over some drums.

The same mama who thought
silence was golden now bends

over laughing when we play,
a smile on her face.

An early birthday wish I never
thought would come true.

It's Weird

being excited to go to
school so I can see Asa
again, so I can know for
sure . . .

Are we friends?

Are things any better at her home?

If I invite her to celebrate my birthday, will she come?

I have to wait because Asa still isn't
in school after the long Easter
weekend on

Monday . . .
Tuesday . . .
Wednesday . . .

and by Thursday, I've
got that feeling again that
something isn't right.

I could tell Mrs. Dial or
ask Mr. Arnold, but

with spring recess
starting next week,
neither choice feels like
the right one.

First Thing Friday

morning I walk to school
like usual, but don't stop.

I keep going to Calumet Street.

The door is wide open, the steps
a sheet of ice, Asa huddled on her
living room floor, her life scattered
about like a loose drum set that
has lost its music.

Asa's mother stomps toward me
when I enter. I dodge her to reach
Asa.

I *remember you!*
Nobody invited you here.
Get out!

Asa sits in a ball in the corner,
shivering beneath a thin sheet,
the purple-blue bruise on her
left cheek still fresh.

A*sa, tell her who* I *am. Tell her we're friends.*
A*sa! We have to go,* I say, trying to pull her to her feet.

Asa snatches her hand away
when two smaller kids trail
into the room one by one,
eyeing me like I'm the danger.

I *can't*. I *can't*. I *can't*.

When her father appears
from another room, I know
better than to stay, to keep
trying to help when the
answer is clear.

I run from the house on
Calumet Street, legs tight
and burning, past my school
and playground where kids
point and call my name, all
the way back home to wake
Mama up with my tears.

Why aren't you at school?

It takes three tries, I'm so out
of breath, heart thumping, mind
spinning, before I can mumble,

There's something I have to tell you . . .

PART III

Drum Roll, Please

April 14

I Tell Mama

Asa needs help. My friend Asa's in trouble.
You need to call the school. You need to call now!

I spill everything I know about
Asa's situation, Zee's heart,
Papa Zee's mail, Mr. Sanderson's
offer in one long sentence that never
seems to end until I run out of air
and collapse.

Mama pulls me close, wraps
both arms around me, doesn't
say a word until she's sure there's
nothing more.

She calls the school to tell Mr. Arnold
where I am, what I said about Asa.

When my breathing has settled,
she tucks me in tight like a caterpillar
cocooned in her comforter.

I'm Trembling

so much the covers
fall away, my eyes dart
around the room focusing
on anything but Mama.

Am I in trouble?

Mama catches my eye,
holds my gaze until she's
ready to dive into the messy
pool of choices I've made.

Not trouble. But let's start from the beginning.
Not about Asa. About Zee.

There's a whole storm of emotion
brewing on Mama's face when I
share the truth about Zee . . .

Surprise . . .
Alarm . . .
Anger . . .
Sadness . . .

She runs her fingers through her locs,
then takes my face in both her hands.

She pauses, eyes piercing,
words clipped.

This wasn't your fault. Do you hear me?
I know you would have done anything for Zee.
He was your best friend. Life doesn't always make sense.
I can only imagine how hard it was for you to keep your word.

I hold my breath.

But delivering Zander's mail? What were you thinking?
Not only is it illegal to tamper with mail, what if something
*   happened to you?*

I exhale, ready to defend
my choices even though it's
clear they weren't the best.

But, Mama, if I hadn't, things would have been worse.
For Papa Zee. And Asa.

Yes, you helped them, but if something happened to you . . .
Promise me you won't ever do something like that again.
When something isn't right, tell me or Mrs. Dial or even Robin.

At the mention of Robin's
name, a smile creeps across

Mama's face, like clouds
breaking way in the sky.

I run to my room to get the flyer
that Mr. Sanderson gave me
about lessons the day I stood
onstage for the first time.

Here. I'm ready. For the next level.

I burrow deeper beneath the covers
while Mama makes her second call
of the day.

There's No Guessing
what happens now for Asa,
when she'll come back to school,
if she'll ever talk to me again
after telling her family secret.

I only know I didn't let what
I knew go unspoken.

Not this time.

Every Morning

after I've shared the truth
with Mama, I trek to Calumet Street,
hoping for a glimpse of Asa, but
the house is dark and still,
no signs of life at all.

Every evening I pour all
my nervous energy into
practicing my drums, helping
Mama find new recipes to bake.
Today makes the strangest
Patriots' Day ever on the eve
of another trip around the sun.

Happy Birthday

to me, I've made it
another year, and
turning twelve feels
bittersweet.

I wake early and ease
across the hall, place
my ear against Papa Zee's
door, already knowing there
will be no hint of music.

Zee would have been turning
twelve soon too. It's still hard
to believe how much has changed
in almost four months since he's
been gone.

Mama, Robin, and me gather around
a homemade carrot cake lit
with twelve rainbow candles.

If things were different
with Asa, I would have invited her.
I make a wish for her to
be okay when I blow out
my candles.

Mama bought me a shiny
red drum set with brass
cymbals instead of Papa Zee's
silver ones and donated his set.

Robin got me my own
subscription to *Drum!*
magazine, and the first
issue arrived with a female
drummer on the cover,
Cora Coleman-Dunham.

I add her to my bedroom wall.

I have two more gifts
to look forward to, making
this the most unforgettable
birthday yet.

First Day After Break

I wake up late,
dress quickly, high-five
my Drum Mavens on my
bedroom wall—

      Sheila E. . . .

    Terri Lyne Carrington . . .

      Cindy Blackman . . .

    Nikki Glaspie (double high-five) . . .

      Cora Coleman-Dunham—

before grabbing the breakfast
Mama left me to eat on the go.

I make it to my classroom moments
before the late bell rings. Asa is back,
her hazel eyes watching me as I rush
to my seat.

All morning long I keep
sneaking glances at her,
leaning closer, trying to
sense whether she's angry.

At lunch I ask to join her,
grateful she doesn't resist.

This time she has a lunch of
her own, although she still
poaches the apple from
my tray.

I smile. She doesn't.

I tell her all about my birthday,
my weekend plans.

She says nothing at all.

I tell her what Mrs. Dial shared
with me about loss and change
and things being different but
not always bad.

When I run out of things to say,
I wait for the bell to ring, take our
trays to the disposal area.

When I turn on my heel, I find
Asa staring, eyes brimming with
tears, reaching out for a hug.

After School

I expect Asa to rush away
like before, but she waits
for me after the last bell.

We're with a foster family a few blocks away.
Close enough to walk here. No more school bus for now.
At least they were able to keep us together.

We huddle by the side
of the building, staying clear
of an arctic blast of wind.

The weather in Boston is so weird.

You're not mad? That I told someone?

Asa darts into the wind and twirls
around like a girl without a care in
the world.

No.

At the start of the school year,
Asa said she wanted one thing:
to get her last badge.

The year's not done yet.
There's still time to try for
your First Aid badge.

Asa spins harder, laughing out loud,
teetering to the ground with dizziness.

Yup!

I lend her a hand, pull her
to standing. The first drops
of rain start and freeze as
they fall.

Even in April it's hard to shake winter.
We're both shivering and unprepared,
so we take shelter at the school
entrance to wait for this to pass.

Zee Is Buried

deep in the cemetery, around
winding curves and small hills,
the sun high in the sky leading
the way.

I notice the daffodils have broken
ground and bouquets of cut flowers
rest on the plots of loved ones we pass.

The soil is muddy from this week's
rain and my feet sink with every
step. We arrive at the black
granite headstone with metallic
gold streaks that blaze when the
sun hits them at just the right angle.

ZANDER ELLIOT ELLIS JR.

MAY 18, 2011—DECEMBER 21, 2022

MAY HE MAKE MUSIC FOR THE ANGELS.

Mama gives my hand an
extra squeeze before she
wipes her eyes, blows her
nose, steps away to lean
against a towering oak tree
so I can talk to my best friend.

You wouldn't believe all that's happened.
Or maybe you do if there's a heaven.
Robin isn't so bad. Neither is Mr. Sanderson.

Wish you were still here, bragging about all your dreams.
You'd still be the best, outplay the rest. No doubt.

I sit down in the mud
next to the headstone, wrap
my arms around the cold granite
even though Mama gives me
a look from where she stands.

I know how fussy she
is about cleanliness.

I'm still playing the drums. Wasn't sure I would again.
Still think we could have made a great band but . . .

Mama gives me a head nod,
telling me it's time.

I have to go now, but I'll be back.
I won't forget us, Zee.
Won't forget our dreams.
Won't forget you.

I kiss the headstone, then wipe
my eyes. Mama and I start toward the
parking lot.

This was the first gift of the day,
there's a second awaiting me.

Drum Roll, Please!

Mr. Sanderson bellows
before the row of drummers
lined against his basement
wall. The class before mine
finishes their lesson with a
crescendo.

As my class waits, all twelve
of us antsy to start, I count how
many girls: five, including me.

Before we take our place
behind a kit as instructed,
Mr. Sanderson hands each
student a set of earplugs that
we will wear during the
lessons.

When Mr. Sanderson offers mine,
he holds my gaze, whispers so
only I can hear him in the noisy
transition between classes.

I've been waiting for this day since Zander first told me about you.
He said be patient, you'd be ready to take it to the next level soon.

With a quickness I slip the plugs
in my ears, give thanks for Zee

always believing in me, and offer
my new teacher a slight smile
before he moves down the row.

With so many girls in the class,
I wonder if we can play together,
maybe form a band.

Has there ever been a band of drummers?

We each take our place. It's finally
happening for me, this opportunity
to get better, work harder, get closer
to my dream.

Author's Note

THROUGHOUT THE YEARS, I've read several news articles about young people who have experienced sudden cardiac arrest (SCA), similar to what Zee experiences in the story. A seven-year-old boy playing tee ball collapses at bat on the field. A nine-year-old girl running through an amusement park to get on a ride goes into cardiac arrest. A twelve-year-old student in the middle of an exam loses consciousness and falls out of his chair, unresponsive. I've always paid special attention to these reports because of my own personal experience at age six losing a very close friend to sudden cardiac arrest. This event left an indelible impression on my childhood.

In many cases, a young person dies suddenly, leaving behind stunned family members and friends. Sometimes there are symptoms, such as chest pain, irregular heartbeats, shortness of breath, and fainting, but sometimes there are no symptoms at all. SCA is rare in children, and according to the Centers for Disease Control and Prevention (CDC), about two thousand young and otherwise healthy people under age twenty-five in the United States die from SCA each year. Without immediate action, like administering CPR and calling 911, SCA can be fatal.

If you or someone you know experiences heart-related symptoms, such as shortness of breath, chest pain, or fainting, please speak up. The CDC recently established a Sudden Death in the Young Case Registry for babies, children, and young adults up to age twenty. The goal of the registry is to help create a better understanding of how often and why SCA happens in young people—and to help learn how to prevent it.

For more information, visit SDYRegistry.org.

Acknowledgments

EVERY WRITER I know navigates the peaks and valleys of the creative journey with the guidance and support of a dedicated group of champions. Humans who have read early drafts, not-so-early drafts, and near-final drafts; made introductions; opened doors of opportunity; extended invitations to lunch; hosted me in their homes for holidays and self-imposed writing retreats; answered emails; did the talking for me when I was too terrified to speak words; created opportunities for me to speak about my work; accepted impromptu phone calls and Zoom meetings; offered words of encouragement; suggested road trips to clear my mind; handed me books for inspiration; and created moments of pure joy and laughter to heal my soul. And so, so much more.

This book would not have been possible without my amazing life partner, loyal family members, and devoted longtime friends who have believed in me as a writer for decades without ever seeing evidence of my work in the world. I am deeply grateful for all the champions in my life, especially Lanita Foley (my Beloved); Charlotte Sheedy (literary agent extraordinaire); Kelsey Klosterman; Ally Sheedy; Stacey Barney (fierce editor who saw the potential in this story from the start), Caitlin Tutterow, Liz Vaughan, and the rest of the amazing team at Nancy Paulsen Books; Erin Robinson, who made the amazing cover art; Natasha Ortiz-Fortier; Jacqueline Woodson; Alex Gino; Tami Charles; Nic Stone; Kacen Callender; Amina Luqman-Dawson; Brigham Fay; Teresa Burns Gunther; Alexia Hudson-Ward; Toni D. Green; the Women of Words Writing Group (Autumn Allen, Janaea Eads, Michelle Chin, Karra Barron, Catherine Boyd, and Yesenia Flores Díaz); the Boston KidLit Drink Night Crew (you know who you are!); the Boston Grub Street Writers of Color Group; and the 2023 Debut Sistars Group.

I always knew I would write a story about a young girl who suddenly loses her best friend. Before I reached the age of twenty, I had lost two best friends and one very close friend. At age six, it was sudden cardiac arrest. At age ten, it was a hit-and-run accident. And at age nineteen, it was a traffic jam gone awry. While this story is otherwise fictional, I do hope readers of all ages find the value in being brave, resilient, and compassionate even when life doesn't go as planned.

It's been quite the journey so far, and I've got nothing but gratitude for it.